SO-CFZ-829

The Education
Of
Queenie McBride

by

Lyndsey D'Arcangelo

WALKER MEMORIAL LIBRARY
800 MAIN STREET
WESTBROOK, ME 04092
(207) 854-0630

Published by
Publishing Syndicate
PO Box 607
Orangevale, California 95662
www.PublishingSyndicate.com

The Education
Of
Queenie McBride

Copyright 2012 by Lyndsey D'Arcangelo

Cover and Book Design: Publishing Syndicate
Edited by Theresa Elders

Published by
Publishing Syndicate LLC
PO Box 607
Orangevale, California 95662

www.PublishingSyndicate.com

Print Edition ISBN
978-0-9850602-4-4

EPUB Digital Edition ISBN
978-0-9850602-5-1

Library of Congress Control Number
2012939705

Printed in Canada

All rights reserved.
Published in the United States
by Publishing Syndicate LLC

*This book is dedicated to
all those individuals who
make a difference
in the lives of
LGBT homeless teens.*

Sometimes the most important
education happens
outside of the classroom.

CHAPTER 1

Pudge stared through the clear glass window into the Burger King on the corner of Harvard and Brighton avenues and licked her dry, salty lips as the smell of grease hit her nose. Bringing her hands to her eyes, she squinted through the glass of the fast food restaurant and looked around. A five-year-old girl sitting near the window happily raised a fist full of fresh French fries into the air and shoved them into her mouth, much to her mother's disgust. An old man with neatly combed silver hair sat in the corner drinking a cup of hot coffee, reading the newspaper. He looked up briefly in Pudge's direction, and then quickly turned away.

Pudge drew back from the window, still salivating, and walked a few feet down the dusty sidewalk. She sat on the concrete and rested her back against a brick wall. The cardboard sign next to her feet read: "Please help. Homeless and need food. Parents kicked me out because I'm gay." But no one seemed to care.

Her stomach growled in frustration, and a slight gurgle of ironic laughter escaped her lips. Before she became homeless, Pudge was a little on the chubby side. That's why all of her friends called her "Pudge." It wasn't meant to be mean or spiteful or anything, just a term of endearment. Nicknames are funny like that. Some of them are hard to explain; others are quite obvious. But in most cases, they do seem to stick to the person they are given to without rhyme or reason. And they tend to stay stuck even when they no longer are relevant anymore. Pudge was anything but chubby these days. In fact, she was thinner than she had ever been in her entire life.

Her stomach growled again, and Pudge winced from the pain. It was just past two in the afternoon and she hadn't eaten all day. The last time she'd eaten anything was yesterday morning, when that nice lady in Boston Common gave her a half-finished bag of popcorn. Boston Common was a great place to scrounge for a bite to eat, because there were so many food vendors around and lots of people willing to give a teenage girl the benefit of the doubt. But she eventually had been chased away by a policeman for begging. Harvard Avenue would have to do for now.

After sitting on the sidewalk for a good hour, Pudge had seen only one person nice enough to give her some change. She jingled the coins together in her pocket as the warmth of the afternoon sun offered her some sympathy. She tilted back her head and closed her eyes.

"Get any money yet?"

Pudge looked up and blinked blindly into the sunlight. Her friend Sam was standing directly over her.

"Not really," she said, reaching into her pocket and pulling out some change. "I collected thirty-six cents."

"That's not even enough for a burger," he said sourly. "Come on, let's go."

"Where?"

"To meet up with Chris."

"I thought he got arrested?"

"Nope. He outran the cops this time. He's laying low for a little bit in South Boston. There's this abandoned building he's been sleeping in, and it's kind of cool. There's room for us, too."

"Don't you want to go back to the shelter?" Pudge asked, hoping to sway him.

"Uh, no. It'll be more fun hanging with Chris. Come on—I bet he even has some food."

Pudge's stomach growled once more as it twisted itself

into a painful knot. She wasn't a fan of Chris, because he was always getting into trouble on the street. But her hunger was getting the best of her. And what she needed most right now was something to eat.

Against her better judgment, Pudge climbed up from the sidewalk and picked up her sign. "Let's go."

CHAPTER 2

"Will you get up already?"

"I heard you the first five times," Queenie grumbled from beneath the covers of her bed. The morning sunlight had already begun to filter into her bedroom, despite the fact that the shades were drawn.

"Then why are you still in bed?" JJ continued. She yanked aggressively at the shades, lifting them up all at once. "It's not a lot of fun having to act like your mother all of the time."

"Then stop. You're a horrible actor, anyway."

"Okay, if you want to be late for class again, then fine. But starting off your college career by going out and clubbing every night probably isn't the smartest thing to do."

"Five more minutes," Queenie groaned, tugging a pillow over her face.

"Are you kidding me, Queenie?" JJ yelled, throwing her hands wildly into the air. "This isn't high school anymore. You aren't going to be able to coast through your classes like you did at Sampson Academy. You actually have to open a book or two. We're in college now, remember?"

"How could I forget that fact when you remind me several times a day?"

JJ jumped on Queenie's bed and snatched the pillow away from her face. "I don't get you lately. Here you are, a freshman at Boston University, one of the best schools on the East Coast. You're hundreds of miles away from your parents and you're living in a fun city with your best friend. Why would you want to throw that all away by flunking out?"

Queenie glared up through sleepy eyes. "You know, if this whole writing thing doesn't work out for you, a career in motivational speaking is a good back-up plan."

"Oh, thanks very much, I'll keep that in mind," JJ said. She jumped off the bed and scooped up her backpack from the floor. "Do whatever you want to do. I'm done trying to light a fire under your butt. I can't be wasting my time trying to wake you up every single day. I have to get going or I'll be late for class myself. I won't be home until later, 'cause we have a writing workshop scheduled with a local author tonight."

"Sounds exciting."

"It is, actually. Don't forget to lock the door this time when you leave."

"Yeah, yeah."

Queenie rubbed the sleep from her eyes and snorted at the irony of the situation. She was the one who suggested they go to college in a big city in the first place. They'd already spent four long years at a small private high school in rural Virginia, and she felt that they needed a change of scenery. They needed to spread their wings, get out and experience the world.

Maybe she was being a *little* lackadaisical when it came to the actual college part, but that was just temporary. She'd get her act in gear eventually. When she and JJ both had been accepted to Boston University, they couldn't wait to move to Boston and start college together. But now that they were here, it seemed as though JJ (otherwise known as Josephine Jenkins, loyal best friend, writer extraordinaire and levelheaded voice of reason) was the only one taking the college part seriously. For JJ, college presented a golden opportunity to take her writing aspirations to the next level. For Queenie, college was an afterthought, a nuisance, basically something to do during the day.

In high school, Queenie always had been able to get good grades without ever picking up a book or having to study before a test. But now the workload and reading requirements for her classes were unreal. How could she have any fun in a big city like Boston when she was supposed to hunker down in the apartment every night and read endless chapters from boring textbooks? She'd have no life outside of the apartment. Besides, she was already behind in almost every class and the semester had just begun. At the rate she was going, she'd probably flunk out by midterm.

After lying in bed a few minutes longer, Queenie finally got up and wandered over to the window. Her eyes stung from the aggressive morning sunlight as she squinted down at the crowded city streets below. She wondered where everyone was going in such a rush. She frowned at the scene and then gave a passing glance at the digital clock on her nightstand. 8:35 A.M. Whether JJ liked it or not, Queenie would be late for class again.

Considering her time constraints, Queenie decided to skip the shower. She fumbled around in her closet, threw on some warm-up pants and a sweatshirt, tied her long unwashed golden-blonde hair back with a rubber band, grabbed a granola bar from the cupboard and headed out the door. She nibbled on her breakfast as she shuffled past strangers on the street. Most of them didn't acknowledge her presence, and those who did wrinkled their faces in disgust. But she didn't care. What did they know? They were too wrapped up in their own real world rat races to realize that she was expressing her individuality by rebelling against societal norms. Or something profound like that. Whatever.

As usual the subway stop was overcrowded, so Queenie shoved her way through to the opposite side where everyone waited for an inbound train. She checked to make sure she was at the correct stop this time, since she'd been prone to accidentally hop on the wrong train. Then she turned up her iPod really loud to block out the street noise. By the time she boarded the train, arrived at the appropriate classroom building and found herself in front of her class door, she already was more than forty-five minutes late.

Queenie knew she wouldn't be able to sneak in unnoticed. An introductory course, sociology was a lecture hall class. About a hundred diligent students sat listening intently as Professor Duncan paced in a tight circle at the front of the room, raising his baritone voice every other sentence in order to keep their attention.

Tyler Duncan was a handsome man by anyone's standards, even though he must be at least forty years old. A Brad Pitt look-a-like, complete with dirty blond hair and a five o'clock shadow, he wore the standard college professor uniform—brown corduroy pants, a button-down shirt with an outrageously colorful tie, and square-framed black glasses.

Queenie was about to give up on her James Bond mission to sneak into class and instead go hang out in the student union, when Professor Duncan managed to circle his way over to the door and open it right in front of her. Queenie stood there as if she were a five-year-old who had just been caught stealing from the candy jar.

"Are you joining us or planning on studying from afar?"

"The view isn't so bad from out here," Queenie replied, without missing a beat.

"Trust me. The view from the front row is much better." Professor Duncan motioned for her to enter the room and then turned around to address the class. "Consider this a simple lesson in social interaction," he said, smiling. "A witty exchange between professor and student, if you will."

As the class laughed, Queenie seized the moment and bowed as if she had been late on purpose simply to demonstrate his point. She took a seat in the front row near the window and set her notebook on top of the desk.

"Now, where were we?" Professor Duncan said, and then cleared his throat.

Queenie's mind began to drift. She stared out the window at the tall buildings and gray concrete that surrounded the campus and began to reminisce about Sampson Academy. She didn't miss the small town atmosphere or her classes. What she missed most was the simplicity and familiarity of high school. She hated the fact that she was no longer a big fish in a small pond. She was a small fish among many other small fish in a very big pond. And this pond wasn't as carefree and fun as Queenie originally had thought it would be. Everyone was so serious all the time. They all had majors, goals, jobs and extra-curricular activities to attend to. They knew exactly what they wanted to "be" when they graduated, and that's all that they seemed to care about. Even JJ knew what she wanted to do after college. As for Queenie, she had no clue. She had never thought that far ahead. There was never any reason to think about the future. At Sampson, she had been so preoccupied with JJ, her friends, basketball, socializing and throwing her parents' money around, that there wasn't any time to think about what she wanted to do with her life. Now everyone around her appeared to have this college thing figured out, while she was busy floundering like a fish just to keep her head above water.

"Now, let's see . . . Queenie McBride, now that's an interesting name. Why don't you, Ms. McBride, enlighten us with your thoughts on this discussion?"

"Huh?"

"Your thoughts," Professor Duncan repeated. "You do have thoughts, don't you?"

The class laughed again, and Queenie shifted uncomfortably in her seat. "Of course I have thoughts," she said. "I just don't have any thoughts on this particular subject."

"Really? None at all?" He smiled at her in a charming yet condescending way. "I would think that a responsible student such as you would be able to contribute something to an open conversation about the reading assignment from last night."

Queenie felt the eyes of the entire class zero in on her but she kept her attention focused on Professor Duncan, who was waiting patiently for an answer.

"I plead the Fifth," she said, coolly.

"The Fifth?"

"Yes, the Fifth. As in the Fifth Amendment?"

"I know what the Fifth is," Professor Duncan replied, his voice a little less playful. "I just wasn't aware that this was an introductory law class. I thought we were in sociology." He walked over to his desk and pretended to shuffle some papers around. "Apparently, I'm correct. This is sociology." He looked up at Queenie. "If you aren't able to handle something as simple as a reading assignment, Ms. McBride, then maybe you need to reevaluate why you're attending college."

"Maybe it has nothing to do with me," she replied, daringly. "Maybe you're just a lousy teacher."

Professor Duncan ignored her and deliberately cast his eyes at the clock on the wall. "Looks like that's all we have time for today, folks. I'll see you on Friday. Make sure you read the entire second chapter so that we can continue this discussion next time without any needless interruptions." He made sure that he was looking directly at Queenie. She acted as if she hadn't noticed.

As the classroom began to empty, Queenie tried to blend in with the rest of the students as they proceeded for the door.

"Ms. McBride, can I see you for a moment?"

Queenie winced and broke away from the rest of the pack. She shuffled woefully over to Professor Duncan's desk, anticipating a lecture of some sort, a little anecdote on the importance of being on time and respectful during class, or perhaps some long-winded monologue about how she should apply herself to her studies and not waste her parents' money—blah, blah, blippity-blah.

"I see right through you," he said instead.

"Huh?"

"That's a choice word in your vocabulary," Professor Duncan chuckled. "You should try mixing it up a little bit. Maybe go for a 'what?' or a 'hmmm?' every once in a while?"

"What?" Queenie asked, happy to oblige.

"As I was saying, I see right through you. There's more to Queenie McBride than meets the eye. You're smart and witty—I'll give you that. But you aren't as confident as you'd like people to think. In fact, I'd venture to say that you're feeling downright insecure and lost at the moment. And you aren't used to that at all."

"Insecure? Me?"

"Yes, you. I propose that everything in your life has been somewhat easy up to this point, especially high school. But college has completely taken you out of your comfort zone, and instead of dealing with the adjustment head-on, you'd rather avoid taking responsibility altogether. I know it seems easier to do it that way. But the consequences aren't worth it."

"You're wrong," Queenie maintained. "I don't know what you're talking about. I think you may have me confused with some other student, because I'm definitely not insecure and I'm not avoiding anything, either. You don't know anything about me. The truth is I've never been more secure than I am at this very moment."

"I know more about you than you think."

"Like what?"

"For starters, I know that you come from a private school in Virginia, and that your parents make a pretty good living."

"How do you know that?"

"Remember the sheet I asked everyone in class to fill out at the beginning of the semester so that I could get to know my students a little better?"

"Oh, yeah," said Queenie, wishing she'd fibbed a little bit when she filled out the questionnaire. "But just because you read a short answer about my background on some piece of paper doesn't mean you know me. It just means you know certain things about me."

"I'll grant you that. Even so, I found your answers to be compelling. It will be interesting to see you evolve and grow throughout the semester. Bear in mind that lots of students go through an adjustment period when they first start college. Don't let it overwhelm you. In order to get something out of it, you have to be willing to put some effort into it." With that, Professor Duncan turned around and began gathering up his things.

"So that's it? I'm not in trouble?"

"This isn't high school, Ms. McBride. This is college, which means personal responsibility and accountability. If you're late for class or you fail to complete an assignment, then you miss pertinent information. And that's on you. I don't care if you pass or fail. I'm not the one paying your tuition bill. All I can do is teach you what I know, and give you a platform from which to grown and learn. What you do with that opportunity is entirely up to you."

With a briefcase in one hand and a bottle of water in the other, Professor Duncan left. Queenie remained at the front of the room, entirely confused. She stood all alone in the empty lecture hall, wondering whether she should feel insulted, angry, relieved or amused. But one specific question ricocheted in her mind.

What if he were right?

* * *

Pudge had managed to collect enough change to take the bus out to Dorchester that morning, which she tried to do at least once a week. That's where she lived—or where her parents lived. They rented the first floor of a double on Foster Street. The outside of the house was painted red, and there was a porch with a bright white railing on the front. Pudge used to sit on the porch and read all day during summers, and her mother would bring her tall glasses of lemonade when it was really hot outside.

The porch was empty when Pudge arrived. She stood across the street, leaning against a streetlight with chipped green paint. It was midmorning and both of her parents were at work. She only stopped by during the day, so that her parents wouldn't see her standing there. Sometimes, she even dared to sit on the front steps of the porch thinking about waiting until her mother came home so that she could talk with her. But after an hour or so, she'd start to get nervous. She'd be afraid that her mother would only turn her way again. Then she'd have no home to go to, ever. At least this way, there was still a chance they'd change their minds. And someday, Pudge knew, she'd get up enough courage to knock on the door and ask them if she could come home. She'd be ready to hear their answer. But until that day, she was content to stand across the street and reminisce about the days when her parents didn't know she was gay and they loved her unconditionally.

CHAPTER 3

JJ didn't get home from her writing workshop until after eight that evening, and by then Queenie had already had her fill of reality television. She was lying on the couch in the living room with her face squished in the side of a pillow and a red quilted blanket draped over her head like a nun's habit.

"Please tell me that you went to class today," JJ said as soon as she saw the motionless lump on the couch. "And that you didn't spend the entire day watching soap operas and reruns of the *L Word*."

"I went to class," Queenie snapped from underneath the blanket. "So stop nagging me."

"Geez, what's wrong with you?"

"Nothing."

"Nothing?"

"Nothing."

"If it's nothing then why are you lying there with a blanket over your head, sulking like a little kid?" JJ sat on the floor next the couch and began to eat the Chinese takeout she had bought at the restaurant around the corner from their two-bedroom apartment.

Queenie sat up and removed the blanket. She still hadn't showered, and her golden-blonde hair was messed and sticking out in all different directions.

"Do you think I'm insecure?" she asked.

JJ almost choked on her orange chicken. "Insecure? You?"

"Yeah, me."

"Why do you ask?"

"Because some numb head professor of mine told me

today that I am insecure."

"So what? Since when does Queenie McBride care what some 'numb head' professor has to say? You're the coolest lesbian I know. Partly, because you don't care what anyone else thinks about you."

"That's exactly what's bothering me. For some reason, I do care and I can't figure out why."

"I don't get you lately. When we first arrived in Boston you were all about it. You couldn't wait to begin college. But you've been acting differently ever since classes started. I don't understand."

"Maybe my professor is right after all. Maybe I am feeling insecure about being at college and that's exactly the reason why I'm acting this way."

"What do you have to be insecure about?"

"I don't know. Do you ever miss it?"

"Miss what? Sampson Academy?"

"Not just Sampson. I'm talking about high school and everything about it. Do you ever miss the way things used to be? How easy everything was? How our biggest concern was who we were playing in our next basketball game, or whether THE incredibly popular and beautiful Kendal McCarthy liked you or not. I never had to study or worry about what I wanted to be when I grew up. I could do what I wanted and have a good time. But everything is different here."

JJ set her food aside and got up from the floor. Without saying a word, she sat on the couch next to Queenie. This was an awkward situation for JJ—seeing Queenie in such a vulnerable state was rare indeed. She wasn't quite sure what to say.

"I'm not used to this."

"Used to what?" Queenie asked.

"Picking you up off the floor and cheering you up. Normally, it's the other way around. But I'll give it a shot.

The truth is I thought I'd be the one who'd have a hard time adjusting, especially with Kendal going to college at Barnard in New York City and me being so far away from home. But I wanted to try and make the best of it. Unlike you, I always had to study hard to get good grades at Sampson. And now that we are in college I have to study even harder. Maybe you need to put in a little more effort. We aren't in high school anymore. You can't expect things to be as easy as they were before. You can still have a good time, there just needs to be a healthy balance between work and play."

"I know."

"*Do you?*"

Queenie paused. "What's that supposed to mean?"

JJ sighed. "I hate to say it, Queenie, but you're all about the 'play' side of things. You've never really cared enough about anything to put in any real work."

Queenie didn't bother arguing. She knew JJ was right. Since she had never had to work for anything in her life, now that she had to, she didn't know how. Her parents were wealthy so she could buy anything she wanted, anytime she wanted. She was athletically gifted, so she could play any sport well with little practice. She had an incredibly good memory, so she could get good grades without studying. And when it came to girls, well, she hadn't ever been in a serious relationship before, so she wouldn't even begin to know how to "work" at it. Girls seemed to attract to her like magnets to a refrigerator because of her charm and humor, but she never let anyone get beyond that. And as soon as things started to turn serious or complicated, Queenie moved on to the next girl.

"You're probably in a little funk, that's all," said JJ when Queenie didn't respond. "What do I know? I've got my own issues to deal with." She picked up her food container and fork, and began to eat again.

"You know a lot," said Queenie. "You're my best friend. You know me best. And you might be on to something. Maybe I am in a funk."

"Then the question is—what's it going to take to make you snap out of it?"

Queenie thought long and hard but couldn't find a definitive answer. She looked down and examined her flannel pajama pants and red-hooded sweatshirt with maple syrup stuck to her sleeve from last Tuesday's spontaneous pancake breakfast. As she ran her fingers through her hair and felt the oily tangles, a look of disgust formed on her face.

"I can't believe it's come to this," she said, rising up and tossing the blanket aside. "Look at me. I look disgusting!"

"I was going to mention that but I didn't want to hurt your feelings." JJ grinned.

"I can't go on like this," said Queenie. "I guess it's time I started to put some effort into this college thing before my parents see my grades and yank me out of school altogether."

"That's right," JJ said, swinging her fork for emphasis. "You know how many of our friends would love to be in your position. Your parents are paying for your entire college, which means no school loans. Don't blow it."

"Okay, I get it," Queenie said as she stood up from the couch. "I'm not going to sit here and wallow in this puddle of self pity any longer. It's about time I started taking college more seriously. I don't want to live off my parents for the rest of my life. Besides, it's beginning to affect my social life."

"If you flunk out your parents may not allow you to live off them for the rest of your life. They might cut you off altogether."

Queenie winced. "That would never happen."

"Never?"

"I mean, I've pulled some pretty ridiculous stunts before. Remember all those private schools I got kicked out of when

I was younger? They've never cut me off before. They've always just bailed me out."

"You were a kid then. Now you're an adult. What if this time, they don't bail you out? Do you really want to wait and see if that happens?"

"Of course not."

"You have a chance to do something about it before it's too late. Get your grades up and figure out what you want to do with your life. Then you won't have to worry about whether or not your parents are going to bail you out when you make a mistake. You'll be able to just handle it yourself."

Queenie's frown slowly morphed into a smile, and she began to laugh.

"What?" JJ asked, trying to remain serious. But Queenie's laugh was contagious and JJ broke into smile.

"I was just thinking about the comment that I made this morning, you know, about you being a motivational speaker and everything. I think you should consider it. Seriously."

JJ shook her head and smiled. "I need to start taking my own advice before I go handing it out to strangers."

"I think I'm going to go for a short walk around the city," Queenie said as she stretched her long body. "I need to get out and clear my head a little bit." She reached for her retro leather jacket, which she had carelessly left on the floor next to the couch. "Do you want to come with me?"

"I can't," said JJ. She picked up the empty food container and stood up. "I have an early class tomorrow and I still have a lot of reading to do tonight. I also want to give Kendal a call before it gets too late."

"Okay. The last thing I want to do is get in the way of you and THE Kendal McCarthy."

JJ pointed her fork in Queenie's direction as she zipped up her leather jacket. "May I make one small suggestion before you head out the door on your journey of self-reflection?"

"Sure."

"Take a shower first."

Queenie sniffed at her armpit and scrunched her nose, "Yeah, that's probably a good idea."

"Insecure? Queenie?"

"That's exactly what I said." JJ stretched and yawned as she held her cell phone up to her ear. "It sounds like an oxymoron."

"Maybe she's just having a hard time adjusting to college," said Kendal. "I know I am. Everything is so fast-paced and intense. It's a definite change from life at Sampson Academy. Remember how it took us only five minutes to walk across the entire campus?"

"I know what you mean. I'm having trouble adjusting to college, too, but at least I'm trying to make the best of it. I didn't tell Queenie about my problem though, because I was too busy trying to make her feel better. She's been in a really bad funk lately, and I didn't want to make it worse."

"I think everyone our age goes through an adjustment period when they go to college. Especially when you move from a small town private school to a big city college like we did. We'll feel differently after a few more weeks, even Queenie. It just takes some getting used to. How's everything else? Do you like your classes?"

"I love my classes, even though they are packed with students. I feel so insignificant, you know? But at least I'm learning a lot."

"What about your writing classes?"

"That's a different story. I was so used to getting praise for my writing back in high school that the criticism I'm getting now is catching me by surprise. It bothers the heck out of me, because it makes me feel like I'm not as good of a writer as I thought."

"But don't you need criticism in order to grow as writer?"

"I guess so."

"What about reading your stuff out loud? I'm sure you don't have any problems doing that anymore."

JJ smiled into the phone. "I haven't actually had to read anything out loud yet. But I'm sure I'll be fine if it ever comes up. I have you to thank for that. You helped me get over my stage fright."

"We helped each other out, remember? You tutored me in poetry and I helped you feel comfortable enough to share your writing with other people. Speaking of which, the Women's Studies program here at Barnard is incredible. There's so much more to study and learn about besides poetry . . . ."

Kendal's sweet voice blended nicely with JJ's nostalgic thoughts. After graduating from Sampson Academy, they had seen each other almost every day over the summer. But lately their communication was reduced to e-mailing, texting and talking on the phone. She missed lying on the grass during those mild summer afternoons, reading through volumes of Emily Dickinson's poetry together. She missed the look in Kendal's eyes whenever they were together, she missed the touch of her hand upon her own, but mostly, she missed the thrill of simply being next to her.

Somehow, things had shifted since the end of the summer. The feelings between them just weren't the same. Like it or not, the distance was affecting their relationship. After all, how were they supposed to be together if they could never actually be *together?*

"JJ? Are you there?"

"What? Yeah, I'm here. It sounds like you're really happy at Barnard."

"I always knew I wanted to come to New York City, but now that I have an idea of what I want to study and major in, it's all falling into place. Barnard is everything I thought it would be and more. It's perfect."

"Yeah, perfect."

"Are you okay?" Kendal asked.

"I'm fine," JJ lied. "I still have a lot of reading to get through, that's all. I should probably get going before I start stressing out."

"Will you call me tomorrow after you're done with classes?"

"Sure," said JJ.

"Have a good night."

"You, too." JJ paused, "Kendal?"

"Yeah?"

It was right there on the tip of JJ's tongue, everything she wanted to say and more about the way she had been feeling about their relationship lately. But something held her back from actually saying it.

"Never mind," JJ muttered. "I'll talk to you tomorrow. Have a good night."

CHAPTER 4

Queenie sat down on the bright green grass of Boston Common and fiddled with her cell phone. The Common, which Queenie initially had been surprised to learn was America's oldest park, was filled with snack vendors, runners, walkers, students, nannies pushing baby strollers, skateboarders, street musicians and break-dancers, and homeless vagabonds. For most of them, it was a just an average Saturday afternoon.

But for Queenie it was something of a blur. So much had happened since she'd made the decision to explore the city the other night and set out for her walk. So much, and she hadn't had time yet to figure out what to do next. She knew she had to do something.

She punched in the numbers 9-1-1 more than a few times but couldn't bring herself to hit the "send" button. It was a ridiculous notion. After all, what would she say? That she bumped into a homeless teenager and was worried about her? They'd ask her to come down to the police station and fill out a report or say something on record. Maybe she could just make an anonymous tip instead? Of course, if she called from her cell phone they could just trace the call.

"Why do these things always happen to me?" Queenie muttered to herself. She threw the cell phone down beside her and fell onto her back. A soft but chilly breeze traveled the length of her arms, tickled her face and ruffled her hair.

All she had wanted was a simple chance to go for a long walk in the city and to breathe some fresh fall air. But it didn't go as planned. Instead of clearing her head and finding herself, Queenie had found Pudge.

She closed her eyes and pictured the bony young teenager in her mind. She could still smell the oily scent that lingered around her auburn hair, and could still see her dirt-stained face, her grungy gray sweatshirt, and the insatiably hungry look in her pale green eyes. The name Pudge hardly fit. Pudge was a tiny, frail little girl who looked as though she hadn't had a decent meal in a month. Maybe two.

Queenie hadn't notice her at first as she'd walked along the sidewalk, taking in the sights of the city. Rounding a street corner, she'd carelessly shambled through a pile of scattered newspapers, cardboard and discarded trash.

"Watch where you're going!" Pudge had barked from beneath the heap.

"I'm sorry," Queenie had replied instantly. "I didn't see you. Are you okay?"

"I was before you stomped right over me with your big, fat feet."

"I said I was sorry," Queenie bit right back. "What in the world are you doing outside, anyway? It's late and you don't look more than twelve."

"I happen to be fourteen," Pudge declared. "I'm just small for my age."

"Twelve, fourteen—what's the difference? You shouldn't be out so late on a school night."

"Says who?"

"Says most of society. Do you live around here? I can walk you home."

Pudge had simply rolled her eyes and laughed.

"What's so funny?" Queenie asked.

"What, are you blind? I live right here. My parents kicked me out at the beginning of the summer. I've been living on the street for about three months now, so you don't have to worry about me being outside on a school night. I can take care of myself."

Queenie placed her hands steadily out in front of her. "Okay, let me get this straight. Your parents kicked you out? As in out into the street?"

"Isn't that what I just said?"

"What in the world did you do?"

"Oh, right. Like it's my fault? It's something I did? Let me guess—you probably think I'm on drugs, right? Or better yet, that I stole money from my parents? That's always a good one. Most people assume that I just ran away anyway, as if I wanted to be homeless or something."

"I didn't mean that at all," Queenie had said earnestly. "I just figured that—I mean I know how it is when you don't always get along with your parents."

"You don't know anything," Pudge grumbled.

"Look," said Queenie, obviously frustrated, "I don't want to get involved in your personal business or anything. I'm sorry for running into you and your, uh, house." As she turned to walk away, she kicked a piece of cardboard. Queenie bent down to pick it up, and immediately saw what Pudge had written on it in big, black bold letters.

"Is this for real?" she had asked, holding the sign in her hands.

"Yes," Pudge said quietly, somewhat embarrassed. She relaxed her stare and added, "I wouldn't make something like that up."

"Let me just clarify this," Queenie continued with a baffled expression, "Your parents kicked you out of the house because of your sexuality?"

"That's what the sign says, doesn't it?"

"What happened?"

"I don't know, really. I finally got up enough guts over the summer to tell my parents that I was gay and they told me I was no longer allowed to live at home anymore. I had nowhere else to go, so I started living on the street. I've been homeless ever since."

"I can't believe parents would do that."

"Well, some do. At least mine did."

"Do you sleep out here every night?"

"Not every night. There's a drop-in homeless shelter on Boylston Street that I go to from time to time. It's not so bad. I can come and go as I please, and they give us food and cots to sleep on. It's a lot better than sleeping on the hard concrete. And everyone there is really nice."

"You're handling it so well," Queenie had said in amazement. "I'd probably be a mess right now if I were you."

"What choice do I have?" Pudge replied. "I have to take care of myself somehow. The only thing that sucks is that I can't go to school and I miss my friends."

For the first time in her mouthy life, Queenie had been at a loss for words. She looked around—taking in the grimy sidewalks, the towering buildings, the busy streets, the endless stream of moving cars, everything—for what seemed liked the very first time since she had been living in Boston. This was it. This tiny concrete section of the city was where Pudge "lived."

Sure, Queenie had a tumultuous relationship with her own parents. She liked to provoke them and get under their skin a little bit. But despite their differences, she still loved them. After all, they had put up with all of her juvenile antics and the fact that she had gotten kicked out of numerous private schools before Sampson Academy. And not once did they ever throw her out of the house, even when she had pushed them to the very limit of their sanity. She couldn't imagine what being cast aside by your very own family would feel like, and she also knew she didn't possess even an ounce of the courage that Pudge apparently had in order to survive on the streets. And here she was, still taking her parents, and their cushy bank account, for granted.

"Are you hungry?" Queenie had asked, spotting a Burger King across the street.

"I could eat," Pudge said evenly, as if the simple thought of some greasy French fries wasn't making her mouth water considerably.

"Come on, I'll buy you a cheeseburger. You look like you could use one."

Pudge chewed on the inside of her cheek. "You're serious?"

"I take it you aren't offered free cheeseburgers on a regular basis?"

"Loose change is more like it. But even that's hard to come by."

"Well," said Queenie, "today is your lucky day. I've got more than loose change on me. In fact, I've got enough money to buy you ten cheeseburgers if you want." When Pudge didn't move, she tugged at her ratty sweatshirt. "What's the matter? Don't you trust me?"

"Why should I?" Pudge declared. "I don't even know you."

Queenie leaned forward on her toes and stuck out her palm, "I'm Queenie McBride, at your service."

Pudge stared at the empty palm. "Queenie? That's your *real* name?"

"I suppose you have a better one?"

Pudge shrugged. "Everyone just calls me Pudge."

Queenie measured her new companion from the side. "Really? Pudge?"

"I was kind of chubby before I was kicked out," Pudge admitted. "The name just kind of stuck."

"Okay, then. Now you know who I am, and now I know who you are. How about that cheeseburger?"

Pudge still didn't move.

"No strings attached," Queenie pressed as she started

walking slowly along the sidewalk, "I promise. After we eat, I'll be on my merry way." She stepped off the curb and started to cross the street. Pudge hesitated for a moment, and then began to follow cautiously.

"I know why you are doing this," she said once they reached Burger King.

"You do?"

"You feel guilty about just walking away and leaving me standing there empty-handed."

"Maybe a little," said Queenie. "But there's more to it than that."

"Like what?" Pudge asked.

"Like the fact that I, too, happen to be gay," said Queenie. "Buying you something to eat is the least I can do."

"Where are you?" JJ asked, cradling her cell phone against her ear.

"I'm sitting at Boston Common taking in some sun on this nice and breezy fall day," Queenie replied. The memory of her meeting with Pudge vanished as soon as the phone rang "Why?"

"You've hardly been around all weekend."

"I have stuff going on."

"What stuff?"

"Just stuff."

"Your parents called here about an hour ago. They said that they tried your cell phone but that it had been turned off. They were a little concerned because they haven't heard from you all week, so I got worried."

"You worry too much," said Queenie. "I was just doing some thinking."

"About what?"

"The ironic side of life."

"Huh?"

"Never mind. What are you doing now?"

"Not much. I've been watching television all morning and I've seen the same three commercials at least five times. Either that or I'm hallucinating."

"I think you need a dose of fresh air. Want to meet me at Faneuil Hall Marketplace? The sidewalk acts are always good for a bit of mindless entertainment. Maybe the cross-eyed juggler with the pointy ears will be there again."

"Wow, the cross-eyed juggler?" JJ feigned excitement. "How could I possibly pass up something like that? I need to take a quick shower first. I'll be there in a bit."

Queenie closed her cell phone and slid it in her back pocket, but not before turning it off once more, just in case her parents tried to get hold of her again. She debated long and hard whether or not she should tell JJ about Pudge. But what would she say?

After they had finished their meal at Burger King the night they met, Queenie had tried to give Pudge some money because it was the only way she knew how to help. But Pudge wanted nothing to do with charity or "pity money" as she called it. It was too easy to take money from Queenie and it would mean that Pudge wasn't able to find money on her own—even if it meant begging on the street. Queenie thought it made no sense at all and figured that it was really a matter of pride.

They parted ways in front of the Burger King sometime after ten, with Pudge heading back to her cardboard palace and Queenie taking a long walk back to her cozy little apartment with its smooth hardwood floors and vaulted ceilings. JJ had been asleep in her bedroom when she got home, and Queenie spent the rest of the night tossing and turning, wondering about the welfare of a homeless teenage girl she hardly knew.

In the past few days, she purposely even had walked by the very same Burger King, hoping to run into Pudge again. But she was nowhere to be found. After a day or so, even the cardboard boxes and newspapers had been cleared away.

An overwhelming sensation of guilt greeted Queenie every morning as soon as she looked at herself in the mirror. She wanted to take Pudge shopping and buy her some new clothes, maybe even get her cleaned up a little bit. She had plenty of money at her disposal to do so. Her parents wouldn't even blink twice at the extra charges on the credit card bill. But how was she ever going to find her again? Boston wasn't exactly a small city. She could be anywhere.

As Queenie walked across Government Center on her way to Faneuil Hall Marketplace, she wondered what Pudge was up to at that very moment.

"I don't know if this is such a good idea," Pudge said. She was crouched down on her knees, in the middle of a circle with a few other kids who also lived on the streets. They were busy planning their next big heist in a deserted alley behind a few apartment buildings.

"Come on," complained a blond boy with a tiny scar on his left cheek. "It's the best idea because no one will expect it. I'm sick of sitting on the street corner, begging for money. No one ever pays attention to us, and all we ever get is a couple of bucks. What good is that?"

"But it's Saturday," Pudge protested. "There's going to be a lot of people there. Somebody is going to see us for sure. They'll call the cops. We'll all get caught."

"Even if someone sees us, they won't be able to catch us."

"But what if they do?"

"You're such a baby."

"I am not," said Pudge, adding a rough edge to her voice. "I'm just not dumb enough to try and steal money in the middle of a huge crowd like you are."

The blond-haired boy sneered at her, and then hit Sam on the shoulder. "You brought her here with you. You make her go along with the plan. I'm doing this with or without you two."

Sam turned his soft green eyes toward Pudge, ruffling a hand through his patch of unkempt red hair. He was so hungry that he could gnaw off his own arm. "Come on," he pleaded. "I'm starving. Chris is right, how else are we going to get enough money for all of us to eat?"

"I don't know," said Pudge. "There's got to be a better way than this."

"Like what?"

Chris leaned over, waiting for Pudge's response. She glared at him, got up from her knees, and dragged Sam off to the side of the alley. "Why don't we just go back to the shelter on Boylston Street?" she suggested. "We can get something to eat there and it's free. We don't have to steal and risk getting into trouble. Chris is bad news and you know it. Let's ditch him now while we still can."

Sam looked over his shoulder to make sure Chris wasn't eavesdropping. "I already promised I'd help him out with this. I owe him for letting us crash at the abandoned house the other day. Remember?

Pudge frowned.

"Maybe we can get enough money to eat for a couple of days," said Sam. "Besides, the shelter is always so crowded."

"Yeah, but it's better than a jail cell," Pudge reminded him.

"Come on," Sam whined. "You heard Chris. We aren't

going to get caught."

"This coming from a kid who gets arrested more than Lindsey Lohan?"

Sam laughed.

"Are you two in or are you out?" Chris demanded as he rose to his feet. "I'm sick of waiting."

"I'm not going to do it," Pudge declared. "I'm going to the shelter instead."

"I promise that this will be the last time," Sam pleaded once more. "I won't make you come with me to help Chris ever again."

Pudge wavered for a moment, feeling the overwhelming urge to just walk away.

"Please?" begged Sam. "I'll even go back to the shelter with you afterwards."

"Fine," Pudge replied, shaking her head. "But as soon as we get the money, I'm out of here. I don't want to do this stuff anymore. I don't care if you come with me or not. But I'm done."

"Okay," Sam nodded. "Come on, let's get it over with."

A popular tourist attraction and outdoor mall, Faneuil Hall Marketplace was packed to the hilt. Queenie had to push her way through crowds of tourists so that she could get a better look at the hip hop dancers who were performing for tips and cheers. Unfortunately, the cross-eyed juggler was nowhere in sight. She found a small open space next to a group of out-of-towners frantically pointing their cell phones at the dancers, snapping pictures.

Queenie marveled at their enthusiasm then made her way over to the tip jar and dropped in a ten dollar bill. Just as it landed on top of the pile of coins and cash, a group of kids rushed by and stole the jar right in front of her.

"Hey," she yelled after them. "Give that back!"

They took off running, scattering in all directions. The crowd dispersed as the dancers broke from their routine and gave chase, and Queenie had no choice but to join them. She ran after the girl who had grabbed the jar, and spotted her jetting down an alley toward State Street in the middle of the Financial District.

"Stop!" Queenie yelled, sprinting down the pavement with blazing speed. Once she'd been a nationally recognized sprinter at Sampson Academy, but had given up running to play basketball with JJ during their senior year. It was easy for her to catch up to the girl, who could barely run while hanging onto the jar.

"Give me back the jar!" Queenie shouted as she reached out and grabbed the back of the girl's gray sweatshirt. "It's not yours to take."

The girl came to a sudden halt and nearly fell over onto the street, desperately trying to catch her breath. She turned around and reluctantly handed the jar over, still breathing heavily.

"Pudge?" Queenie asked in amazement. "Where have you been? I've been looking all over Boston for you the past couple of days."

"Well, you must have not been looking too hard," Pudge huffed in between breaths. "I've been around."

"Why did you steal money from the street performers? And who were those other kids?"

"They're just kids who live on the streets like I do. We took the money so we could get something to eat."

"That doesn't make it right."

Pudge raised a cold shoulder. "If I could dance, I would do that for money instead. But I don't know how to dance.

So, this is what I have to do."

"I tried to give you some money the other day and you turned me down."

"I told you, I don't need your charity."

"Obviously you do, if you have to steal the money instead," Queenie reasoned.

"What do you want from me?"

"I just want to make sure you are okay." A gust of wind gathered up in the alley and circled around them. "You can't keep living on the streets. It's going to get cold soon and you'll freeze to death. Let me get you a hotel room or something."

"Why do you care so much? Just because you're gay doesn't mean you know what I'm going through."

Queenie was about to argue when someone yelled, "That's her!" She turned around and watched as the group of dancers and a policeman on horseback came toward them at full speed.

"I can't get arrested," Pudge said quickly. "They'll call child protective services on me."

"But maybe that's exactly what you need."

"You don't understand! If they call child protective services on me then they'll make me go to a home or put me in foster care. I don't want to do either."

"But—"

"If you really want to help me like you say you do, then don't let me get arrested."

Queenie peered over her shoulder. She had less than a second before the angry mob of dancers would be upon them.

"Please," Pudge begged.

Queenie swallowed hard as the dancers surrounded them in a tight circle. "That's her," one of them pointed at Pudge with a mean finger. "She's the one who took our money."

The policeman dismounted his horse and retrieved the tip jar from Queenie's hands. Then he reached over and forcefully grabbed Pudge by the arm.

"Wait," said Queenie. "She didn't take the money. I did."

"I saw her take the jar," said one of the dancers. "You chased her down for us. You were trying to help us get it back."

"No," Queenie lied. "That was the plan. See, I told her to take the jar and give it to me once we reached the alley. I don't even know her. She's just an innocent pawn in my devious scheme. I enjoy ripping off street performers for fun."

The policeman considered Queenie's story with a furrowed brow. Then he turned to Pudge and stared her down with steely eyes. "Is that true? Did she tell you to take the jar?"

Pudge gave a slight nod and kicked at the pavement.

"Why did you listen to her?" the policeman asked.

"Because she promised that she'd buy me a cheeseburger."

"What kid would turn down a cheeseburger?" Queenie added. "It was like taking candy from a baby."

The policeman found little humor in Queenie's response. He handed the tip jar back to the hip hop dancers and told Pudge that she was free to go.

"You're going to have to come with me," he said to Queenie, as he radioed for a patrol car to come and pick her up.

"Can I make a quick phone call?" Queenie asked, searching for her cell phone in her back pocket.

"Don't push your luck. I know you lied to cover for that girl."

"Why would I do a foolish thing like that?"

"I'm standing here wondering the exact same thing. You seem like an intelligent young woman." The police car pulled up and he opened the door to the backseat. "They'll let you use the phone once you get to the police station. Let's go."

CHAPTER 5

"You're in jail?" JJ asked incredulously.

"That's right," Queenie answered. "What can I say? I'm a regular thug."

"What in the world did you do?"

"It's a long story. I just called to let you know where I was so you weren't running all over Faneuil Hall Marketplace looking for me. It was just a simple misunderstanding, that's all. I'll be home at some point, and I'll explain everything then."

Before JJ had a chance to say anything else, Queenie hung up the phone and winked smartly at the overweight policeman who was sitting across the desk from her.

"Thanks for letting me make my one phone call," she told him.

"You can make more than one," he replied as he sipped from a mug of steaming coffee. "You're not under arrest."

"Well, that's a relief. I wouldn't want to blemish my perfect record."

"The dance group isn't pressing charges. We just needed to fill out a report about the incident and then I'm supposed to send you off with a warning. But something tells me that you aren't the repeat offender type."

Queenie leaned forward in her chair, "How can you be so sure? I have quite the checkered past, you know."

The policeman smiled in amusement and bit into the pumpkin-flavored muffin he was holding. "Can I ask you an honest question?"

"That depends. Can I answer freely without a lawyer present? I've watched plenty of *Law and Order* episodes, so I know how these things work."

"Why did you cover for the runaway who really stole the tip jar?"

"What makes you think I covered for her?" Queenie replied, trying to look innocent.

"I read the report. The officer on the scene seems to think you took the fall so that the other girl could get away. And from the looks of you, I tend to agree. You don't appear to be hard up for money."

Queenie glanced down at her clothes. She was wearing a platinum timepiece with real diamonds on the face, her favorite retro leather jacket, designer jeans and a fresh pair of black leather boots.

"One of the dancers even saw you drop some money in the tip jar before it was taken," the policeman added. "So your story doesn't really add up."

"Okay," Queenie admitted. "You got me. I did put a little money in the tip jar. But then I realized that I needed it back. So I panicked and took the whole thing instead. It was all just a huge misunderstanding."

"You're pretty quick on your feet." The policeman chuckled. "And though your explanation seems highly unlikely, if that's what you want us to believe, then so be it. I would like to offer one word of advice, however. Don't make a habit of covering for other people's crimes. It might not always work out the way you want it to. You seem like a good kid, and it would be a shame if you ended up in jail for something you didn't do." He pointed at the front door. "You're free to go."

Queenie nodded, thanking him with her eyes and letting him know that she had understood him clearly at the same time. When she exited the building, she wasn't surprised to see Pudge waiting for her outside on the front steps.

"Well, well . . . look who it is. Maybe we should change your nickname to 'sticky fingers' instead of 'Pudge.' It's fits much better."

"Ha ha," Pudge replied, crossing her arms. "Very funny."

"I'm just saying," said Queenie. "If the criminal route is the one you want to take, you might as well have a nickname to go with it."

"I don't need a lecture, okay? I know what I did was wrong. I just wanted to thank you for covering for me. That was, you know, kind of a cool thing to do."

"Some might say it was a stupid thing to do, but I'm known for doing stupid things now and then." Queenie looked up and down the street. "Where are you off to now? Did you eat yet?"

"Why? You want to buy me another cheeseburger?"

"Maybe."

"I don't need another cheeseburger, or anything else that you want to buy me. I can take care of myself."

"Really? From the looks of things you aren't doing too good of a job of it."

"If it wasn't for you, I wouldn't have gotten caught in the first place."

"If it wasn't for me, you'd be sitting in a jail cell right now, waiting for child protective services to arrive."

"All right," said Pudge. "I get it. But you don't have to feel guilty anymore. This is the second time you've helped me out, so you're off the hook."

"I don't feel guilty," Queenie maintained. "If anything, I feel responsible."

"Why? You hardly know me."

"I don't really know why," Queenie continued. "The reason doesn't matter. Why don't you come back to my place? You can get something to eat, take a nice hot shower and spend the night. It's warm and free."

"No, thanks," said Pudge. "I'm crashing at a shelter tonight. I've got to get going. I'll see you around."

"At least let me walk you there," said Queenie. "I have to go that direction, anyway."

When Pudge didn't put up a fight, Queenie skipped down a few steps and joined her on the sidewalk. After walking a few blocks in silence, they arrived in front of the Boylston Street homeless shelter.

"You'd rather stay here than at my place?" Queenie asked, taking in the exterior of the building, which looked rundown and shoddy.

"It's not so bad," said Pudge. "I can come and go as I please."

A thin young woman approached them as soon as they stepped into the foyer. She was dressed in ripped blue jeans and a fitted black sweater. Her shadow black hair was cropped short at a sharp angle and tucked back behind her ears, revealing a pair of doe-like brown eyes. Queenie couldn't help but notice them.

"Pudge!" she cooed.

"Hey, Izzy."

"I was hoping you'd make an appearance today. You're just in time for dinner." They exchanged a quick hug. "Who's your friend?"

"I don't know," Pudge pretended. "She sort of followed me here, mumbling to herself along the way."

"At least they were coherent mumbles," Queenie added. "I'm Queenie McBride. Good citizen at large. I just came along to make sure Pudge got here safely."

"Nice to meet you. I'm Izzy Mancini. I work here at the shelter as the volunteer coordinator." She tousled Pudge's hair. "I'm also in charge of coordinating daily activities for our teenage drop-ins."

Pudge ducked out from under her reach.

"It's almost dinnertime," said Izzy as she checked her wristwatch. "Do you want to stay and eat with us?"

"No, thanks," said Queenie. "I'm just dropping off the goods."

Pudge gave her a look and happily retreated to the next room.

"Thanks for bringing her here, really," said Izzy, once Pudge was out of earshot. "I worry about her whenever she's gone for more than a few days. She can come and go whenever she wants to since we're only a drop-in center. Sometimes, kids never come back again."

"It's no problem at all."

"Just out of curiosity, how long have you known Pudge?"

"Not that long, actually. I ran into her a week or so ago on the street and I've been trying to help her ever since. But she won't take my money, or anything else that I offer. She's one stubborn girl."

Izzy narrowed her eyes. "She's not stubborn, she just knows better. A few measly dollars won't get her off the streets."

"Yeah, but at least it'll help."

"With what, exactly?"

"I don't know. Something?"

"That's the problem with you people."

"*You people?*"

"Yeah, people with money. Money doesn't fix everything, you know? What did you think would happen? That she'd take your money, buy a few fancy things and be okay? She knows that she needs more than money. She needs a friend. She needs support."

"I'm trying to be her friend."

"How? By dropping her off at a homeless shelter? By giving her a few dollars for food?" Izzy placed her hands on her slim hips. "Pudge is just one of hundreds of thousands of gay kids living on city streets throughout the country. You can't buy their way off the street. You can't buy them the kind of family support and love they need and deserve."

"Whoa, calm down a minute," said Queenie. "I didn't know what else to do. I've obviously never been in a situation like this before."

"Well, once you figure it out then let me know," Izzy replied coolly. "We could always use some extra volunteers."

* * *

"Queenie McBride. To what do I owe the honor of your presence?"

"I kind of need to talk to you," Queenie replied with a sheepish grin as she hung in the hallway outside of Professor Duncan's office. It was early Monday morning, and she hadn't been to class in over a week.

"Would this conversation have anything to do with why you've been missing my class lately?"

"I know how it looks. But it's not what you think. I've just had a lot going on lately. Is it okay if I come in and explain a few things?"

Professor Duncan swung open his office door wide enough so Queenie could squeeze through. Then he sat back down in his desk chair and motioned for her to have a seat in the empty chair across from him.

"You let me down," he said bluntly. "I thought that maybe I hit a nerve with you in class the other day, and I was looking forward to seeing how you were going to respond. But as soon as you started missing my class, I figured you for a lost cause."

Queenie's eyes roamed around the office and settled on

one of the framed degrees hanging on the wall. She wasn't used to being upfront with anyone besides JJ. It was hard for her to check her sarcasm at the door.

"You did hit a nerve with me," she admitted after a long pause. "And you were right, I was feeling a little lost and insecure about being at college—about a lot of things, really. I was ready to take this whole college thing by the horns and run with it. But then I got a little sidetracked."

"By the bright lights of the big city?"

"No, by a spunky young homeless girl who, coincidentally enough, reminds me of myself, which makes her all the more infuriating."

"A homeless girl?" Professor Duncan repeated, making sure that he had heard her correctly.

"Yeah, a homeless girl. I basically ran into her on the street one night. She was living underneath a pile of newspapers and cardboard boxes. I've never seen anything like that before. I mean, let's be honest. I'm from a wealthy suburb of Virginia. We don't get too many homeless folks roaming about. And seeing her having to live like that was a shock to my system."

"What did you do?"

"I took her out for a cheeseburger and then we went our separate ways."

Professor Duncan nodded quietly, as if this sort of thing happened all the time. He fiddled with the collar of his pale blue button-down shirt, which matched his pink-and-blue-checkered tie perfectly.

"And now you're feeling guilty about the situation?" he asked.

"At first I was. I even went searching for her. I mean, she's only fourteen years old and all I did was to buy her a burger. I guess I wanted to do something more for her and make sure she was okay."

"The guilt is understandable, seeing as how you come

from a privileged background and it's your first time in a big city environment. But it's important for you to realize that you aren't responsible for her. You don't have to help her because of your own guilt."

"You don't understand. I don't want to help her out of guilt. I know I felt guilty at first, but it's different now. She's so young. And her parents kicked her out of the house because of her sexual orientation. She has nowhere else to go."

"Wait a minute," said Professor Duncan. "This sounds like a serious issue between this young girl and her parents. Maybe you are getting too involved?"

"That's an understatement," said Queenie. "I ran into her over the weekend when she was trying to steal some money for food, and I took the rap for her and got arrested."

Professor Duncan placed his hand on his forehead and massaged his temples. "Queenie, it's one thing to take a homeless girl out for a cheeseburger, but now you're going a little too far. Call the proper authorities so that she can get the help she needs."

"It's not that simple."

"Perhaps, but it's not that complicated either. You've already missed classes because of this situation, and it sounds like you are getting in over your head. I'm sure that your other professors are just as concerned. We're talking about your college education here, Queenie. You have an opportunity that isn't afforded to everyone. It's time to start making it a priority."

Queenie pushed her chair back forcefully. "You know, the last thing I expected from you was a lecture. I came to you because I thought you'd understand. I thought you could give me some advice on what to do."

"I am giving you advice on what to do. Leave it alone."

"I can't. It's like you said—I'm too involved. I can't walk away now." She reached for the office door and heaved it open. "You know, you talk a pretty good game. I thought you were different because you teach sociology. You're supposed to understand these kinds of 'social' situations, right? But apparently you're just like everyone else. You think that if you turn your back, the problem will just go away. But the fact is that the problem will still be there. I know what it's like to be a gay teenager and it's not easy, but at least my parents didn't turn their backs on me. Pudge has to deal with being gay and living on the streets, don't you get that? If I can help her, then that's exactly what I am going to do—even if it means failing your stupid class. How's that for sociology?"

CHAPTER 6

Queenie slammed the apartment door so hard that a book fell off the kitchen counter and onto the floor. JJ came running into the room, dressed in gray sweatpants, a hooded sweatshirt and a worn Red Sox baseball cap.

"Where in the world have you been all weekend? I called your cell phone a billion times but it kept going straight to voicemail. What happened? Are you okay? Why didn't you call me? When did you get out of jail?"

Queenie picked the book up off the floor and passed it over to JJ without so much as glancing in her direction. "Were you this much of a nag at Sampson? I can't seem to remember."

JJ tossed the book aside. "I'm not nagging you, I'm just a little curious as to how one gets arrested in the middle of a Saturday afternoon while strolling innocently through Faneuil Hall Marketplace, then somehow magically disappears for the rest of the weekend? I'm your best friend so I have a right to know these things."

"You are nagging me," Queenie spat as she slid onto the couch and picked up the television remote. "You've been nagging me ever since we moved here because you don't have THE Kendal McCarthy to keep you occupied anymore." She clicked on the television and turned up the volume.

JJ's mouth opened wide with resentment. "I can't believe you just said that to me. What's up with you? You're as emotional as a scorned 50-year-old menopausal woman."

When Queenie didn't respond with her own witty retort,

JJ knew something was seriously wrong. She walked in front of the television and stretched her arms out to further block the screen. She even turned her baseball cap around to let Queenie know she meant business.

"If I recall the last time you did this, I tossed you aside like a ragdoll," Queenie warned.

JJ didn't move. She knew Queenie was much stronger than she was and towered over her petite 5'4" frame. But if this is what it took get to the bottom of whatever was going on with her best friend, she was more than ready to risk a few bruises.

"I don't want to fight with you," Queenie told her. "It's not about you."

"Then stopping acting like a jerk and tell me what happened," said JJ. "Where have you been?"

"After the whole 'getting arrested' incident, I spent two nights in a hotel. I just needed some time to myself to clear my head, okay?"

"Okay." JJ chewed on the inside of her cheek. "Why couldn't you just call me and tell me that?"

"I don't know. I didn't feel like talking to anyone at that point. Not even you." Queenie turned off the television and tossed the remote onto the couch. She stared straight at the wall, at nothing in particular. "I have a great idea for a story," she said. "You're going to love it."

"I already told you that I have no interest in writing your memoir."

"It's not about me," said Queenie. "It's about a homeless girl named Pudge."

"Good name for a character. What's the plot?"

"She's a fourteen-year-old who was kicked out of her house for being gay, and now she's living on the street."

JJ took off her hat and ran her fingers through her hair. "Are you serious?" she asked. "Is this for real?"

"Yes."

"I take it your little stint in the jailhouse had something to do with this."

"As always, you're quite perceptive."

"So, what happened exactly?" JJ asked.

"Remember last week when my professor called me insecure?"

"How could I forget? I've never seen you look so miserable before."

"After you and I had that talk, I went for a walk in the city and ran into Pudge on the street. She reluctantly told me about her situation, so I bought her some food at Burger King because I didn't know what else to do. But ever since then, this little voice in my head keeps telling me I should have done more."

"That would be your conscience speaking."

"Funny," Queenie said dryly. "Apparently, the Universe agrees with my conscience because I ran into Pudge again on Saturday at Boston Common. She was trying to swipe some money from a few street performers, and I caught her. But when the cops came, I took the fall."

"So that's why you got arrested," JJ said, incredulously.

"Yeah, and you don't have to tell me it was a dumb move because I've already figured that out."

"I wasn't going to say anything," said JJ. "What happened after that?"

"Nothing," said Queenie. "I walked Pudge to a homeless shelter and felt good about leaving her there. That was until some pretty employee named Izzy scolded me about my lack of awareness regarding homeless gay teens. She said that I couldn't 'buy' Pudge's way off the street. Then I tried going to my sociology professor this morning for advice, but he threw the whole 'it's-not-worth-messing-up-your-college-career' thing in my face. He thinks I'm getting way too involved."

"He's got a point."

"I've just never dealt with an issue where I couldn't buy or scheme my way out of it," Queenie explained. "I have no idea what to do now."

"That's because you usually don't deal with anything. You are the 'queen' of avoidance. No pun intended."

"Can we talk about something else?"

"Case in point," said JJ.

"It's just frustrating. My professor told me to walk away and do nothing, and Ms. Izzy scolded me for not doing enough. I don't know what to do at this point, but there has to be a happy medium. Think about it JJ—the same thing could have happened to either one of us. What if our parents had thrown us out for being gay? My dad may have said a lot of harsh things to me when I first came out, but he eventually came around. He wasn't as upset about that as he was about all the times I got kicked out of private schools before Sampson Academy."

"You were the master at that, for sure."

"This whole situation with Pudge makes me wonder what would have happened if he hadn't come around. What would I have done? Where would I be now? I don't think I would have been as self-sufficient as Pudge, that's for sure. It's like she has no fear at all."

JJ sat down on the couch next to Queenie. "I don't know what I would have done if my parents had kicked me out, either. It's because they were so supportive that I eventually felt comfortable enough to be myself around other people, too."

"Exactly."

"Where is your new friend now?"

"Pudge? I don't know. She could be anywhere. I was going to go back to the shelter tomorrow to see if she's there. Do you want to come?"

"Yeah, I'll come. I'd like to meet this Pudge character

face-to-face."

"I have to be honest with you. She's a little rough around the edges."

"I'm sure I can hold my own."

"Okay," said Queenie. "But don't say I didn't warn you."

CHAPTER 7

Queenie and JJ arrived at the homeless shelter just after two in the afternoon the next day. Pudge was sitting in the recreation room with a few other kids her age, watching MTV on a beat-up television set that was dented and boxy. When she saw Queenie walk in, she rose up from the couch cautiously.

"What did I do now?"

"What makes you think you did something?" Queenie asked.

"I don't know. I guess I didn't think I'd see you again for a while," said Pudge. "Especially after getting you arrested." Pudge took one look at JJ, placed her hand on her hip and said, "What are you looking at?"

"I told you," Queenie whispered. "Rough around the edges."

"I'm not looking at anything," JJ answered plainly. "I'm a friend of Queenie's."

Pudge studied JJ up and down, as if she were taking notes. By the look on her face, she was hardly impressed.

"This is JJ," Queenie explained. "She's my roommate. I wanted her to come with me to meet you. You know, in case you ever stop being so stubborn and take me up on my offer and stay at my place."

JJ shot Queenie a look.

"We can discuss the particulars later," Queenie assured her. Then she turned her attention back to Pudge. "What are you up to this afternoon? And where's Izzy?"

"So that's why you came by," said Pudge with a sly expression. "You wanted to talk to Izzy?"

"No," Queenie maintained. "I came by to check on you. But if Izzy is here, I might as well say a friendly hello. I didn't make the best first impression on her the other day."

"I don't know where she went. But you can hang out for a little while if you want. We're watching *Jersey Shore* on MTV."

Queenie consulted her watch then whispered to JJ. "Do you mind if I stay. I don't have anything else going on today."

"Knock yourself out," JJ replied. "I've got a few errands and stuff to do today." She turned to Pudge and gave her a slight head nod. "Nice meeting you, Pudge. Maybe I'll see you around sometime."

"I doubt it," Pudge said under her breath. As soon as JJ left, she turned to Queenie and said, "She's kind of uptight."

"Eh, it's part of her nature," said Queenie. "She's cool."

"Cool?" said Pudge, obviously unconvinced.

"Trust me. She's the best friend I ever had."

"Yeah? Why's that?"

"Because she gives me enough room to be myself. She also helps me stay grounded even though I tend to get a little crazy now and then. It's important to have a friend like that in your life, you know, someone who can keep you in line."

"I don't have any friends like that," Pudge said.

"What about the kids you hang out with here at the shelter and on the streets?" asked Queenie.

"They're cool and everything, but I wouldn't call them friends exactly. I mean—they don't keep me in line, like you said. If anything, they convince me to do things that get me into trouble. Like, steal money from street performers."

"I see." Queenie scratched at the base of her chin, pretending to be thinking. "I'll tell you what. I'll be your friend. You know, the kind that keeps you in line and doesn't ask you to commit criminal offenses."

"I'll have to think about it."

"Think about it? You should feel honored that I want to be friends with you. I'm Queenie McBride, you know? I'm practically considered royalty in the State of Virginia."

"Yeah, right," said Pudge. "A royal pain in the—"

"Good morning, ladies."

Queenie and Pudge spun around to see Izzy standing behind them with her arms folded loosely in front of her. She was dressed in a pair of tight-fitting jeans and a tan cardigan sweater. There was a look of suspicion in her eyes, as if she knew they were up to something. It was a look that Queenie had seen before, and she immediately began to wonder if she was about to get scolded once again.

"I was just letting Pudge know that I will be available whenever and wherever she needs me," said Queenie as she placed her arm around Pudge's shoulders.

"Aren't I lucky," Pudge said, forcing a fake smile before she poked Queenie in the ribs with her elbow and retreated into the next room.

"Kids," Queenie said clumsily.

"Did you decide to take my advice after all?" Izzy asked.

"What advice?"

"About offering your friendship instead of a few bucks for a measly burger?"

"Yeah, that's right." Queenie straightened up and smoothed out the sleeves of her leather jacket. "I'm turning over a new leaf. Doing some outreach work and stuff."

"Oh, really? Then I suppose you wouldn't mind sticking around for the sharing session?"

"Sharing session?" Queenie asked, suddenly uncomfortable.

"Relax. I'm not asking you to share anything. It's just a casual conversation I hold for our homeless gay teens. It gives them an opportunity to talk about anything that is bothering them, so that they have a chance to vent. It's nothing official. Why don't you join us? It might help you get to know Pudge a little bit better."

"You think so?" said Queenie. "It's like she's wearing a bodysuit made of iron so no one can get through."

"She's got her guard up, but with good reason. Try living on the street for a few days and see how many people you trust."

"I think I'll stick with the sharing session," said Queenie.

They walked down the hall and into a small room where a group of teenagers sat in an uneven circle. Izzy picked up an empty chair near the back of the room and brought it over.

"Here," she said to Queenie. "Have a seat." Then she turned her attention to the entire group. "Hey, everyone. This is Queenie. She's going to sit in on the sharing session today."

"What kind of a name is Queenie?" asked one boy with a mop top of fiery red hair. He looked as though he hadn't showered in over a week.

"It's the best kind of name," Queenie replied smoothly, "Because I don't know another person in the whole world who has it."

"I happen to like it," said Izzy. "It's original."

"Like my name," said Pudge.

"Your real name isn't Pudge," the boy said. "That doesn't count."

"Of course it counts," said Queenie. "My best friend goes by JJ, even though her real name is Josephine Jenkins. But everyone calls her JJ, so it counts."

The boy sneered at her, "Whatever."

"Sam, since you're so talkative today," said Izzy, "Why don't you go first."

"I don't have anything to say."

"You could have fooled me. I'm sensing anger in you this afternoon. What's going on?"

"Same stuff as always," Sam exhaled with a huff. "My parents are still jerks. And every time I go back home they think I'm going to stop being gay, as if I can turn it off and on like a light switch. I always end up running away again."

"I wouldn't call them jerks," said Izzy. "But I can understand your frustration."

"I would," said Sam. "They don't understand anything about homosexuality. They don't realize that it's something I can't control."

"Just because they don't understand, doesn't mean they are jerks. It just means that they need some time to grow and evolve."

"By the time they grow and evolve I'll be an old man," Sam said bitterly.

"When's the last time you were home?" Izzy asked Pudge in an attempt to redirect the conversation.

"I haven't been home in over three months," Pudge answered quietly.

"Have you thought about going back?"

"No." Pudge lied and sat up straight in her chair. "I don't need my parents. I don't need anybody."

"But you can't keep living on the streets," said Izzy.

"I can if my parents don't want me anymore."

"Maybe it's time for you and Sam to consider other options. We have social workers here who can place you in a group home or with a foster care family."

Sam heaved his shoulders forward and laughed forcefully. "Yeah, right. Why does everyone always act like foster care is so great? I know a kid who is living with foster parents who don't let him do anything or go anywhere. I bet he ends up running away from them, too."

"There are plenty of good and loving foster families out

there," said Izzy. "I know many kids that have come through here and were placed into foster care. They are doing just fine, and they are completely happy with their foster parents."

"Good for them," Sam spat.

"I agree with Izzy," said Queenie, who had been watching the conversation unfold. She twirled her hands in a circle directly at Sam. "You've got a little anger going on there."

"Wouldn't you be angry if your parents kicked you out because you were gay?" he asked. "Who am I kidding? Look at you. It's obvious that you have no idea what we go through. Why are you even here? Once you leave I bet you're going back to your fancy apartment and forget all about kids like us."

"Sam," Izzy cautioned. "Queenie is here because she cares. I understand that you are feeling angry and upset right now. And it's good to talk about it and express it, but it's not good to take it out on other people."

Queenie sat back in her chair without saying a word. She didn't respond because she knew that Sam was right. She had no idea what these kids were going through, and she had no idea what it felt liked to get kicked out of your own home for being gay. The thought was hard to imagine, and even harder to swallow. And yes, she'd probably be extremely angry with her parents—she'd probably be a lot of things. But at that moment, she knew she should shut up and let them do the talking.

"I'm glad that you stayed for the whole thing," Izzy told Queenie as they stood in the foyer after the sharing session had ended. "I know it must have been hard to sit there and listen to their stories."

"I'm not going to lie," said Queenie. "It was intense. I had no idea that this kind of thing happened. I've never met anyone who was kicked out of their house for being gay before. I feel a bit naïve and foolish about it, actually."

"Don't feel foolish," said Izzy. "You'd be surprised at the number of people in this country who have no idea that LGBT teen homelessness is even a problem. They don't even know what bisexual or transgender is, let alone what LGBT stands for. We clearly need more awareness about this issue. We need to get the word out."

"Maybe I should volunteer then, like you said."

"Really? The other day, you couldn't wait to drop a fifty in Pudge's pocket and be on your way."

"That's not true. It's just that I grew up with parents who used money to fix everything. So that's how I thought I could help her. But now I can see that there are other ways, like volunteering."

Izzy open her mouth to speak, but paused. "You're serious about this?" she finally asked.

"I came back again, didn't I?"

"I guess I'm just a little surprised. Volunteering doesn't seem to be your kind of thing."

"How do you know? You only just met me the other day."

"Trust me. I'm an excellent judge of character."

Queenie looked up at the ceiling briefly. "Look, I know that I didn't make the greatest first impression. But I'm not the kind of person you think I am. And if you let me buy you a cup of coffee, I can explain more."

"Are you asking me out?"

"Depends," Queenie said, smiling.

"On what?"

"On your answer."

"You're really full of yourself, aren't you?"

"Come on," said Queenie. "It's only a cup of coffee.

I promise to behave myself."

Izzy hesitated. "All right," she said with a forceful finger. "I'll have a cup of coffee with you. But only because I'm interested in what you have to say and nothing more."

"Fair enough," said Queenie.

CHAPTER 8

"I've never met anyone like you before," said Izzy. She and Queenie were sitting near the window at a corner coffee shop near Harvard Square, sipping lattes.

"Well, that's because I'm one-of-a-kind."

Izzy's eyes rolled on cue. "That's exactly what I mean. You have a smart reply for everything. It's charming, sure. But it also makes me wonder what you're hiding. Like, if you're covering up your insecurities or something."

Queenie laughed. "Do you happen to be related to my sociology professor?"

"What?"

"He pretty much said the exact same thing to me during one of my classes—that I put on a front because I'm insecure."

"Was he right?"

Queenie blew at her coffee cup and let her gaze wander out the window. Then she looked across the table, tracing the base of Izzy's delicate cheekbone with her eyes. "No. I'm not always this confident," she confessed. "I wouldn't even call it confidence, actually."

"What would you call it then?"

"Overcompensation."

"For what?"

"For my insecurity," Queenie grinned.

"Okay," said Izzy. "I'm waiting for your explanation."

"Okay. I come from a very wealthy and ritzy family. People have always bent over backwards to please my parents. Once I was old enough to start making friends, the only reason anyone wanted to be my friend was because my family had money." Queenie sat back in her chair and looked out the window again. "I've always hated my parents for putting me in a situation like that. So I've had this odd obsession to get back at them by spending their money as quickly and frivolously as possible, even though I know it doesn't accomplish anything. They get upset, but they never do anything about it."

"Why don't they stop giving you money?"

"Because they don't look at money as the problem. They look at it as the solution. They've always used money to fix everything. For example, when I was younger I told them I didn't want to go to another private school after getting kicked out for the billionth time. So they bribed me with a BMW. I took it and ended up going to Sampson Academy."

"You didn't have to take the BMW," said Izzy.

"I know I didn't. But I did. Looking back on it, I'm glad I went. I met my best friend, JJ, while I was there. And luckily, she was a good influence on me. I behaved myself long enough so that I could actually graduate. But that's why I'm a nineteen-year-old college freshman instead of eighteen, not because I'm not smart or anything like that. It's because I got expelled enough to get behind a year. But I liked Sampson, so I paid attention and did well. I ran track for a few years, then I played basketball my senior year with JJ. I had a good time at that school. If I hadn't gone there, who knows where I'd be now."

"Sounds like you miss it."

"I do," replied Queenie. "I miss it a lot. But I didn't mean to go off on a tangent about high school. I was just trying to explain about the money issue—it's a hard habit for me to shake, not using money to fix things, because it's what I've done my entire life. As a result, I use money the same way my parents use money. What can I say? They taught me everything I know about spending money. " She looked carefully at Izzy, who wasn't the least bit amused. "You probably think I'm materialistic and arrogant."

"I'm going to be honest with you," said Izzy. "At first, that's exactly what I thought. You have this demeanor about you that can easily be mistaken for arrogance. But now I can see that it's more of a defensive mechanism, because there's a sensitive side to you that you don't want anyone to see."

"Sensitive?" Queenie argued. "No, no—that's JJ's department. She's always been known as the sweet and romantic one. It's in her blood."

"And you play the role of the overconfident player?"

"Hey, I never said I was a player." Queenie sat up in her chair, resting her arms on the table. "I just haven't met the right girl yet."

"Hmmm mmm," Izzy teased, quietly sipping from her cup. "So, tell me, why did it bother you then when your professor called you insecure?"

"I think he saw through my overconfident exterior and it caught me off guard. No one, aside from JJ, has ever called me out like that before. At Sampson Academy, I was comfortable. I knew exactly where I stood. Here, I'm not sure where I fit in, or if I fit in at all. I don't know what I want to do after I graduate, or why I'm even in college in the first place. My professor must have spotted that right away, which either makes him incredibly astute or a closeted superhero with special mind-reading capabilities."

"I'd put my money on astute."

"He even said that he was looking forward to watching me grow and evolve. What teacher says that?"

"Some teachers have a keen eye for these things. And he's right. The beauty of college is that it gives you the time and space to figure it all out and evolve at your own speed."

"Maybe," said Queenie. "Hey, why are we talking all

about me? Let's change it up a little bit. Tell me something about you."

"What do you want to know?"

"For starters, what does Izzy stand for?"

"Isabella. I grew up in a large Italian family." Izzy pointed at her nose, "Hence the Italian beak. Anyway, everyone in my family called me 'Izzy' for short when I was little."

"I like it."

"It's not quite as cool as 'Queenie,' though."

"Trust me, the name comes with the territory," said Queenie. "My parents are Virginia socialites. I guess they hoped their children would turn out the same way if they put the proper names in place. But their plan failed miserably. They ended up with a lesbian delinquent who has a smart mouth instead."

Izzy laughed loudly and a few people in the coffee shop turned to look in their direction.

"I like it when you laugh," said Queenie.

"I like to laugh."

"Tell me something else about you."

Izzy tapped her fingernails against her coffee cup, contemplating what information she was willing to share. "Since you shared something so personal with me, I'll do the same for you—I was homeless once, like Pudge."

"Really?" Queenie slumped back in her chair as if a light bulb had just gone on in her head. "No wonder you're so tough."

"Remember what I said about Pudge earlier? I still have a hard time trusting people because of my time living on the street. You have to toughen-up quickly when you're homeless. I was only a junior in high school when I left home and moved to Boston. I lived with some friends for a little bit before I finally got myself together, got a job, got an apartment and finished high school. Then I enrolled at

Wheelock College. I'm going to graduate this spring with a degree in social work, and I plan on starting graduate school in the fall."

"Wow," said Queenie. "You've accomplished a lot."

"I did what I had to do."

"Do you still talk to you parents?"

"Every once in a while. My friends and coworkers at the shelter are my family now."

Queenie chewed on her lower lip. "Was it because of your sexuality? Is that why you left home?"

"It was a big part of the reason," Izzy explained. "And that's why I am so passionate about LGBT teen homelessness. I know what these kids are going through because I went through the same exact thing. They trust me more because of it. And I feel like I can really make a difference in the outcome of their lives."

"That's amazing. You have this sense of purpose, like you know exactly what you want to do in life."

"I do."

Queenie paused and reflected back on her time at Sampson Academy. "I wish I had that," she said. "I never thought to look past high school. We lived in such a safe and secure little bubble that I didn't have to think about anything outside of it. I was too busy living it up every day to consider what I wanted to do with my life after I graduated."

Izzy nodded once more. "No one ever thinks to look past high school when you're in the thick of it."

"I wish I knew what my purpose was," said Queenie. "Everyone I know seems to have that part figured out already. JJ has always known that she wanted to be a writer and she's so good at it. I have no idea what I want to do with my life. The only thing I'm good at is spending my parent's money."

"I don't believe that for a second," said Izzy. "Everyone is good at something. Part of the discovery just involves going with the flow of life and trusting your gut. My journey brought me here to the shelter. I had no idea what I was going to do when I arrived. But I trusted my gut and things fell into place. I discovered that I love working with homeless teens and that it's something I'm really good at." She pointed at Queenie's midsection. "What is your gut telling you?"

Queenie focused her eyes on her stomach and concentrated. "Right now, it's telling me that I'm hungry."

Izzy laughed. "That's because you're 'thinking' about it and not 'feeling' it. What does your gut feeling tell you?"

Queenie concentrated some more. Then she raised her head and said, "It's telling me I should volunteer at the shelter."

Izzy sat back in her chair and studied Queenie closely. "Stop joking about that."

"I'm not joking," Queenie maintained. "Honest, I really want to volunteer at the shelter. It's a gut feeling. And after everything that I just told you, how can you still not believe me?"

"I want to make sure that you are doing it for the right reasons."

"I told you my reasons already. I'm doing this for myself and for Pudge."

"Right. And getting to know me better has nothing to do with it at all?"

"Now look who's full of herself?"

"Ha," Izzy scoffed.

"This isn't a joke to me," said Queenie as she set her cup down forcefully. "I may have a long history of not taking things seriously, but I'm serious about volunteering. Pudge is a cool kid and I want to be a friend to her. I want to try and make a difference, without throwing money around. I don't know what else I have to do to convince you. I think that I at least deserve a chance."

Izzy's face softened. "Okay, you've made your point. If you're really and truly serious about this, like you say, then come by the shelter tomorrow afternoon and we'll fill out the paperwork." She got up from the table. "I know you think that I'm being hard on you, but I have to make sure that all of our volunteers are genuinely at the shelter to help. This isn't something you can do halfway. You have to be able to give these kids your full attention every time you are there."

"I won't let you down," said Queenie. "I promise."

"It's not me that I'm worried about. It's Pudge. Especially if she opens up to you."

"I won't let her down, either. You can trust me and so can she."

Izzy looked intently at Queenie and nodded.

Queenie smiled as if to say, "I told you so."

"Don't get all cute and confident on me now," Izzy warned. "It's going to take a lot more than a fancy latte and a charming smile to convince me fully. I'll see you tomorrow."

CHAPTER 9

"That Izzy is unlike any girl I've ever met before," said Queenie. She was lying on the couch in the apartment, flipping through the television stations with no intention of stopping on any particular channel. "I smile and nothing happens. She just rolls her eyes at me. And she always looks at me like I've got something up my sleeve, as if she's just waiting to call me out on it."

"She knows you that well already?" asked JJ, who was busy in her bedroom getting dressed to go and pick Kendal up from the airport.

"I was perfectly genuine, polite and sincere when we went for coffee," Queenie stated emphatically. "I even opened up to her a little bit about myself, and you know that's not something I do easily. But it looks like I still have to do a lot more than that in order to prove to her I'm not the person I used to be. That much is obvious."

"Don't be so hard on yourself. You two just got off on the wrong foot, that's all." JJ came into the living room dressed and ready to go. "How do I look?"

Queenie sat up and turned off the television, giving JJ her full attention. "You look a little . . . desperate."

"Desperate?" JJ panicked, looking down at her outfit.

"I'm kidding. You look fine. I'm sure that THE Kendal McCarthy is going to be just tickled pink when she sees you."

"Why do you insist on still calling her that?"

"Because that's what I always called her in high school."

"Yeah, but we aren't in high school anymore. Maybe

that's your problem. You haven't yet grasped that concept."

Queenie shifted in her seat. "What do you mean?"

"Izzy told you she's a senior at Wheelock College, right?"

"Yeah."

"Well, you're just a freshman. There's a huge difference between college freshmen and college seniors."

"Yeah, but I'm not your average college freshman. I'm nineteen, remember? She's only a couple of years older than me."

"I'm not talking about age. I'm talking about the way you act. Sometimes, you can be a bit immature. Like continuing to refer to Kendal as 'THE Kendal McCarthy.'"

"That's ridiculous."

"No, it isn't. I've met a few seniors at school who are in my creative writing class. They're ready to get out in the real world and start their careers, while we freshmen are just trying to figure out how to do our own laundry and get to class on time. It's night and day."

"Maybe you're right," said Queenie. "But that's part of the reason why I decided to volunteer at the shelter. Maybe I can show Izzy that I'm not just some bumbling, immature freshman, and that I'm not as shallow or as materialistic as she thinks I am." Queenie rolled off the couch and marched over to the window. "Who knows, maybe she'll also warm up to me in the process."

"As long as you are volunteering at the shelter for the right reasons, I'm all for it."

"I am," Queenie insisted. "I even sat in on one of the sharing sessions that they have for gay teens the other day. It made me realize a lot of things about myself." She turned away from the window. "Seems like I've got a long list of people to prove wrong—my professor, Pudge, Izzy, even you."

"Queenie, you don't have to prove anything to anybody, least of all me."

"Yes, I do. It's obvious that you still think I don't know how to take anything seriously. Apparently, Izzy and Professor Duncan agree with you. But I'm about to change all of your perceptions." Queenie stuck out her hands and aimed her thumbs directly at the center of her chest. "See the lazy, non-committal, unmotivated, naïve and selfish Queenie McBride you once knew standing before you?"

"Uh, yeah?"

"Take a good, hard look. 'Cause she's about to be replaced with a new and improved version."

"Queenie 2.0?" asked JJ.

"I was thinking something more like the I-Queenie 4000. It has a better ring to it."

JJ waited as patiently as she could in front of the security gate at Logan International Airport, nervously tapping her left foot against the floor. She watched as the crowd of passengers made their way past the security checkpoint, trying to spot Kendal in the middle of the fray.

She'd dressed in an outfit she thought Kendal would like: a pair of dark faded jeans, a long-sleeved cream-colored waffle T-shirt and a pair of Timberland boots. In the middle of running back and forth to class, she'd even found time to get her hair cut.

As she shifted her weight from one foot to the other for the billionth time, she saw Kendal emerge from the sea of passengers, rolling her suitcase close behind her.

JJ stood up on her tiptoes so that Kendal could see her and eased into a relaxed smile as Kendal quickened her pace until she was practically running full speed toward JJ. As soon as they gathered each other up in their arms, JJ felt an electric tingle erupt throughout her entire body. She felt the warmth of Kendal's breath upon her neck and inhaled the familiar scent of her perfume.

"I've missed you so much," she whispered into Kendal's ear. "You have no idea."

They held each other for another minute or so, before Kendal finally broke the embrace. She reached for her suitcase, but JJ had already picked it up.

"I've got it," she said confidently.

"Always the gentlewoman," Kendal remarked.

"You know it."

As they walked through the airport together, JJ noticed that Kendal's hair had grown past her shoulders. There was something else that was different about her, but JJ couldn't put her finger on it. But dressed in skinny jeans and a long-sleeved V-neck T-shirt, she looked just as beautiful as ever.

They hailed a cab right outside of the terminal door and settled in the backseat. JJ immediately reached for Kendal's hand, but Kendal already had taken out her cell phone and begun texting feverishly.

"What are you doing?" JJ asked curiously.

"Texting my roommate to let her know that I got in safely. She's kind of Momish in that way." She giggled, and laughed at the phone. "I've become really close to a few girls who live in my dorm, and they are asking me all of these silly questions about Boston. Just give me a quick sec."

JJ nodded, but kept staring at the phone.

"Is something wrong?" Kendal asked.

"Not at all," JJ lied. "I'm just really happy to see you."

After texting back and forth a few more times, Kendal finally slid her phone back into her purse. Then she leaned over, hooked her arm around JJ's and rested her head on JJ's shoulder.

"I know this whole long-distance thing has been kind of hard," she said. "But let's try to make the best of the weekend, okay?"

JJ mustered a smile and turned to stare out of the window at the clear blue sky. An unsettled feeling had erupted in her stomach as she began to suspect that Kendal was hiding something.

CHAPTER 10

Queenie waited for everyone else to leave the classroom so that she could meet with Professor Duncan one-on-one, only this time it wasn't because she was in trouble. She wanted him to know that she was serious about school and his class in particular. She also wanted to apologize for walking out of his office the way she did the other day.

Professor Duncan acknowledged her presence by directing his eyes at her as she lingered off to the side of his desk. He continued to speak to a group of students in front of him about their current assignment. Once the crowd dispersed, Queenie seized the moment. She pulled up a random desk chair and spun it around so that it landed with its back facing the front of his desk. Then she straddled the seat, resting her elbows on the back of the chair, and leaned forward.

"This must be serious," said Professor Duncan.

"It is serious," said Queenie. "I'm becoming quite the serious student, and I have a serious proposition for you."

"Then I guess I have no choice but to pay *serious* attention to you," Professor Duncan played along and sat down at his desk.

"I know we didn't exactly part ways on the best of terms last time," Queenie started, "but I'm willing to swallow my pride a bit if you are willing to extend an ear in my direction so that I can apologize."

"I think I can oblige. I also want you to know that I understand why you were upset, but you left in such a huff last time that I didn't really get a chance to explain my position clearly."

"I may have overreacted just a wee bit," Queenie said with an apologetic grin. "I know that you meant well, and I completely get where you were coming from. You were just looking out for my best interests. But I may have found a solution that benefits everyone."

"You've piqued my interest. What's the master plan?"

"Funny enough, it actually coincides with the semester project you assigned during class today."

"Researching an important sociological issue with a group and doing a class presentation?"

"Yes."

Professor Duncan pondered the notion. "Okay, I'm listening."

"I have a great idea for the assignment, but I need to do it independently rather than with a group."

"Why is that?"

"Because I plan on making Pudge part of the research and presentation. I'm positive that I can gain her trust and get her to open up to me, but I can't see her doing that with a whole bunch of other students that she doesn't know."

"And who is Pudge, exactly?"

"The homeless girl I met, remember? There are many more kids just like her out there. LGBT teen homelessness is an important sociological issue, but it's hardly discussed in the mainstream media. I want to research some statistics and do my presentation on it. I've already signed up as a volunteer at a youth homeless shelter in the city that caters to gay teens. This way, I'll be able to maintain a friendship with Pudge, do what I need to do for class, and gain some outreach experience as well."

Professor Duncan adjusted his glasses. "This experience has really hit home with you, hasn't it?"

"More than you know."

"All right. I'm going to let you do this, because I think

you've stumbled onto something that's going to make a significant difference in your life. And I'll even let you do it independently. But there's one thing I'm going to ask for in return, one small concession."

"Anything," Queenie replied eagerly. "Whatever it is, you got it."

Professor Duncan placed his hands on his desk, stating his position clearly. "You aren't allowed to miss any more of my classes for the rest of the semester. If you do, I'm canning the project. And you have to be able to stay on top of your other classes as well. Additionally, if the situation with Pudge gets too overwhelming and complicated then you come directly to me for help and we'll call the proper authorities."

"Done," said Queenie without a second thought.

"Well, Ms. McBride," Professor Duncan said as he leaned back in his chair and rested his hands on his lap. "It appears as though you are finally ready to step out of that comfortable little bubble you brought with you from Virginia, and face some new challenges head on. I'm proud of you."

"Oddly enough, I'm proud of myself. It's not a feeling that I'm accustomed to, either."

"May I ask what brought about this evolvement in the first place?"

"Honestly, it was a few things. First, you got under my skin with your little 'insecurity' comments. Then I ran into Pudge, which seems far too coincidental not to be destiny. And then there's Izzy." Queenie shook her head. "I guess it's true when people say that things always happen in threes."

"Who's Izzy?"

"Oh," Queenie waved a casual hand into the air. "That's a whole other story."

* * *

Pudge wandered into Izzy's tiny office and sat down on the edge of her desk. She was wearing a pair of tattered jeans with dirt stains on the knees, muddy Converse sneakers that were once bright red, and a gray hooded sweatshirt.

Izzy looked up from the paperwork in front of her. "Bored?"

"Very," Pudge muttered.

"Well, in a few minutes you can help me set up for dinner."

"How exciting."

Izzy poked Pudge in the leg with the butt of her pen. "How about sitting in the chair instead of on my desk?"

"Fine," Pudge groaned, like the dramatic teenage girl she was. She stood up and plopped her body down in the flimsy white plastic chair in the corner of the room. It was the kind of chair one would find on the front porch of an average suburban home, a bit out of place in an office setting.

Izzy tried to refocus her attention on the work in front of her, but couldn't keep from noticing that Pudge was eyeing her steadily.

"Okay," she said at last and set her pen down. "What's up?"

"Nothing," said Pudge as she picked at a hole in her jeans.

"I know *something* is up. You don't normally come into my office to hang out and chitchat. So spill it."

"I—" Pudge bit her lip. "I miss my parents. I've been missing them a lot, actually. But it doesn't make sense. How can I miss people who don't even care about me?"

Izzy relaxed her stare. "It's natural for you to miss them," she said. "They are your parents. You can't control what they do or how they act. All you can do is accept them for who they are."

"But why? They don't accept me for *who* I am." Pudge twisted her body in the chair and brought her knees up to her chest.

"I've been exactly where you are," Izzy said openly. She rose from her seat and walked gingerly around the desk, kneeling down in front of Pudge. "The challenge for me was finding love and peace for where my parents were at. I still love them, but I don't define myself through them anymore."

"It's so hard," Pudge said, beginning to sob. She buried her face in her arms to hide her tears. "They don't want me because of something that I can't change. If I went back and told them I was straight, they'd welcome me home. What kind of love is that?"

"It's conditional love—the worst kind," said Izzy. She reached out and pulled Pudge's face away from her arms so that she could see her eyes clearly. "It's important for you to understand that love should never, ever, be conditional. Real love is compassionate and without expectation. Real love accepts everyone for who they are."

"So if I don't accept my parents for who they are, then I'm basically doing the same thing to them that they are doing to me?"

"Exactly."

"I don't know how to do that."

"You'll figure it out in time. And once you reach that level of acceptance, you can let go. You won't have to carry the hurt and the anger around with you anymore. You'll rise above it and get the love you deserve from other people instead."

Pudge stared at Izzy with tears in her eyes. "Is that what happened for you?"

"Yes. I have plenty of friends in my life who accept and love me just the way I am. You'll meet plenty of wonderful people who will accept and love you just the way you are, too. I guarantee it."

Pudge looked away from Izzy. "I wonder if they will ever come around, my parents, I mean. I'm not ready to give up on them just yet."

"They might come around. But you don't have to put your life on hold and wait for them to catch up. Look at yourself through your own eyes, not theirs, and see how wonderful and special you are."

"I don't feel so wonderful and special."

"Well, you are," said Izzy. "But it doesn't matter how many times I tell you that. You have to believe it yourself."

"How did you get so smart?" Pudge asked, returning her gaze to Izzy.

"I wouldn't exactly call it smarts," Izzy replied. "I'd call it experience. It does wonders. Not too long ago, I was in the same situation as you are. Look where I am now. Someday, you'll be able to give the same advice that I am giving to you to someone else."

"Someday, I won't have to. Someday, parents will love their kids unconditionally, no matter what."

Izzy smiled warmly and smoothed Pudge's hair, "Someday."

Pudge wiped her face with the sleeve of her sweatshirt. "I can help you set up for dinner now, if you still want me to."

"I'd love for you to help."

"Do you think that Queenie is going to stop by later?"

"I don't know."

"Do you want her to?" Pudge asked.

"Why do you ask, Ms. Nosy?"

"I think she likes you," Pudge declared.

"Oh? How do you know?"

Pudge brushed her shoulder gently against Izzy's and winked. "It's just a feeling I have."

Izzy could feel herself blushing. "I think you're reading into things, just a bit."

"Do you like her?"

"I think she's a very intriguing person."

"What does that even mean?"

"It means, let's stop talking about Queenie and get things ready for dinner. That's what it means."

"Okay," Pudge gave in. "But I still think she likes you." She wagged her head up and down, grinning as she followed Izzy toward the dining area.

CHAPTER 11

JJ and Kendal sat quietly across from one another on the ferry to Provincetown. It was a bright, warm, sunny Saturday afternoon—one of those fall days without a cloud in the sky.

So far, their weekend together hadn't gone quite as smoothly as JJ had envisioned. After she had picked Kendal up at the airport, they went back to the apartment and sat around chatting for a bit before heading out to dinner. Their conversations used to flow as effortlessly as water from a spout, but now they were having trouble keeping the conversation going. It kept stalling like an old clunker trying to make its way up a hill. And JJ felt she had to get out and push a little in order to keep Kendal entertained.

To make things worse, JJ had made reservations at an expensive steakhouse, only to find out that Kendal recently had given up eating red meat. And their "romantic" stroll by the Charles River had been rudely interrupted by a passing thunderstorm. They had spent the night watching a movie with Queenie instead, which was hardly romantic because of Queenie's nonstop burps and chatter. JJ anxiously hoped that a nice relaxing day-trip to Provincetown somehow magically would transform the rest of Kendal's visit into the blissful weekend she had imagined.

"I don't feel so good," Kendal said, interrupting JJ's reverie. She bent over in her seat and pressed her hands against her cheeks.

"I think you might be getting seasick," JJ observed. "Let's go out on the deck so you can get some fresh air."

She pulled Kendal up by the arm and walked her outside of the ferry's cabin. They leaned against the railing and let the fresh air and mist from the water wash over them.

Kendal inhaled deeply and took a few lengthy breaths.

"Feel better?" JJ asked.

"I think so."

"I didn't know you got seasick."

"Neither did I. Then again, I've never been on a boat before."

"You've never been on a boat? Well, you'll feel better once we get there. Everyone here talks about P-town, and how much fun it is. It's like a gay Mecca."

Kendal put on a smile and looked up at the sky. JJ couldn't help but get the feeling that she was wishing she were someplace else.

"Are you okay? Or maybe I should be asking if 'we' are okay?"

"I don't know," said Kendal. "I'm getting a strange vibe from you. I've felt it since I got here, as if something is bothering you and you aren't telling me what it is."

"I guess I'm not good at hiding my emotions."

"No, you aren't. But that's one of the many things that I love about you."

JJ leaned forward over the railing and stared solemnly at the water below. "Honestly, I've been feeling like we're drifting apart. I know that we have two different lives going, and it's hard to stay connected all the time. But I don't even feel connected with you now, and you're standing right next to me. I feel like you'd rather be back in New York with all of your new friends."

"I was afraid this would happen," said Kendal. "We were able to see each other every day back at Sampson, and we got to spend lots of time together over the summer, too. We spoiled each other with constant attention. Even the way we got together was magical; it was like something right out of a novel."

"I know," said JJ. "I think I may have to write a book about it someday."

"But we can't keep trying to recreate that same magic or our history with Emily Dickinson and everything that happened in high school. We have to accept the fact that things change. And we have to flow with it instead of trying to fight against it."

JJ felt the overwhelming urge to protest but she knew that Kendal was right. "So, now what?" she asked.

"I don't know. But I know that we have to stop wishing things were the same as they used to be. Maybe we just need to let go and see what happens?"

"You know me, though. Letting go is a lot easier said than done. I like to know what's going to happen."

Kendal placed her arm around JJ's waist. "And you know me. Meeting you taught me to be open to new experiences. That's why I went away to college in New York in the first place. I wanted to experience something new and exciting."

"Can I ask you something?"

"Anything."

JJ averted her eyes and gripped the railing with both hands. "Have you, um, met anybody?"

"I've met lots of people."

"You know what I mean."

"If you're asking if I've met anyone that I am interested in besides you, then no. But I promise that if I do, you'll be the first one to know. I'd hope you'd tell me if you met someone as well."

"I'm not looking to meet anyone."

"Well, you know what *I* mean."

The ferry station at Provincetown was in plain sight now, and the people scattered along the boardwalk appeared to grow bigger as the ferry approached the dock.

"We can still make the most of today," said Kendal. She linked her arm around JJ's. "We're here together, so let's relax and enjoy each other's company."

"You keep saying that, like everything is going to come to an end afterwards."

Kendal bobbed her head in frustration and dropped her arm to her side. "If you keep acting like this, it will."

JJ winced.

"Just listen to what you're saying," Kendal continued in a softer voice. "You keep focusing on the fact that we can't see each other all the time and that things are different. Instead of just going with the flow and adjusting to the way things are, you're fighting it. It's only making things worse. Why would I want to come visit you if all you did was talk about the way things were back at Sampson Academy, or wonder if I'm interested in someone else, and completely forget the fact that I'm standing here right beside you?"

JJ turned away. "Maybe I am pushing you away because I'm afraid I'm going to get hurt in the end."

"Keep pushing and that's exactly what's going to happen."

The ferry slowed, easing its way toward the loading dock. The boardwalk was crowded, and everyone appeared to be enjoying what could be one of the last sunny and warm days of fall.

"I don't know why, but I feel like I've already lost you," JJ said sadly.

Before she could respond, Kendal bent her head forward and leaned over the railing. At first JJ thought that she was crying, but when Kendal made a loud retching sound and heaved her body simultaneously, JJ quickly realized that she had gotten sick.

"I'll get you some ginger ale," JJ said, darting back into the cabin. When she returned, Kendal was sitting on a bench near the railing with her head thrown back.

"Here," said JJ, sitting down next to her. "We can just ride the ferry back to Boston if you want. We don't have to stay if you're not feeling well."

"Do you mind?" asked Kendal, tying her hair back in a ponytail. "I feel absolutely horrible."

"No, I don't mind," said JJ. To her it was the perfect ending to their disastrous weekend.

CHAPTER 12

"She's right," said Queenie. "But you already know that."

JJ looked at Queenie, who was sitting beside her on the red fuzzy blanket they had spread on the grass at Boston Common. She had left Kendal at the airport after a stale and awkward goodbye, uncertain if they would see each other again before the holidays.

"I know she's right," said JJ. "But it doesn't make it any easier. I want things to be like they were at Sampson."

"Okay, now you're sounding like me not that long ago," said Queenie. "Or don't you remember telling me that we're not at Sampson anymore?"

JJ pulled her Red Sox baseball cap lower over her eyes. Ominous clouds began to gather over their heads, and the air smelled heavy with rain.

"What are you so upset about, anyway?" Queenie asked. "It's not like she broke up with you or anything. You should be happy that she wants to try and make it work."

"I know. But I get the feeling that she would prefer it if we did break up. She said some stuff about us letting go and seeing what happens. To me, 'letting go' is pretty much code for 'breaking up.' It's not like she said she wasn't going to break up with me, either." JJ growled in frustration. "Argh! I'm horrible when it comes to uncertainty."

"JJ, our entire lives are filled with uncertainty," Queenie said calmly. "Get used to it. Nobody knows what's going to happen from moment to moment, no matter what age they are." She picked at the grass then added, "Besides, if I were Kendal, I would have broken up with you before the ferryboat docked back in Boston."

JJ stared at Queenie in total surprise. "Why would you say something like that?"

Queenie got up and stretched her long legs. "I'm your best friend, right?"

"Right."

"And part of the role of being a best friend is to always be upfront and honest no matter what, right?"

"Right."

"Quite honestly, you're not much fun to be around anymore. And the silly part is that it's over nothing. You and Kendal are still together, yet you act like she's already dumped you. You've been moping around like some little lost puppy, and for some reason all you do is complain about everything. What's up with that?"

"I know. It's more than just this thing with Kendal. Maybe I'm taking out my other frustrations on the both of you and that's the real problem." JJ fell on to her back and covered her face with her hands.

"What other frustrations? I thought everything was going perfectly wonderful for you?"

"I'm missafbabggbgle," JJ moaned.

Queenie straddled over her and craned her neck. "I can't understand you when you talk through your hands like that."

"I said I'm miserable!" JJ shouted between her fingers.

"That part is obvious," Queenie replied. She bent down and yanked JJ's hands from her face. "It's the *why* that has me so confused and concerned."

JJ pushed Queenie playfully aside and sat up again. "I didn't want to tell you this because you've had so much going on lately, but I've been feeling a little out of place in this city. To make matters worse, I'm practically flunking my creative writing class."

"How is that even possible? You're a writer."

"I don't know. I have had a horrible case of writer's block, and I can't shake it. My professor says that I'm not producing anything original or authentic. I even tried handing in my famous 'Mother May I?' poem for an assignment, and she called it 'elementary' and 'something a high school student would write.' "

"Well, you did write it while you were in high school."

"I know I did, but it's ridiculous! I'm supposed to ace my writing courses. I'm a writer! It's like a carpenter flunking woodshop."

"You're being too hard on yourself. Stop trying to *be* a writer and just *write*."

"What's the difference?"

"The difference is what you're missing. Instead of writing the things you think your professor will like or that you think she is looking for, write what you know. That's when you write your best stuff."

"Okay, Yoda, got any equally sage advice on what I should do about Kendal?"

"Do nothing. You must," Queenie joked, helping JJ up from the blanket. "Seriously, there isn't anything you can do. Why can't you just enjoy what you have with Kendal while it lasts, and be okay with the outcome—whatever that may be."

"I don't know."

"Come to think of it, in the entire time that I've known you, you've always either been in a relationship or looking for one. Why are you so afraid to be alone?"

"Listen to you," said JJ. "When did you become a voice of reason and rationality on relationships? That's supposed to be my role."

"I've always been the voice of reason where Kendal is concerned, remember?" Queenie gathered up the blanket in her hands and stuffed it into JJ's backpack. "It's like your brain turns into mush whenever her name comes up. Anyway, I was being serious. Maybe you need to be single for a little while."

"Maybe."

They walked along a cement path toward an underground T-station entrance, stopping to buy hot pretzels along the way.

"What are you up to this afternoon?" JJ asked.

"I'm hanging out at the shelter for a little bit. Then Pudge and I are going to go walk around Faneuil Hall Marketplace. I'm hoping that if I spend more individual time with her, she'll open up to me."

"And how are things with Izzy?"

"It's hard to tell. But at least she doesn't put on that tough girl act around me so much anymore. I think maybe I'm growing on her."

"Yeah, like a fungus," JJ replied, smugly breaking off a piece of her hot pretzel and shoving it into her mouth.

"Very funny."

"I thought so," said JJ, with her mouth full. She shrugged, and continued as she chewed, "I still can't believe that Pudge has been living on the streets for the entire summer."

"I know," said Queenie, biting into her own hot pretzel. "Can you imagine how difficult that must be? Even the concept of being able to shower everyday is something I take for granted."

"Forget about showering," said JJ. "What about the stress of having to figure out where your next meal is coming from?"

Queenie considered the half-eaten hot pretzel in her hand. The pair munched in silence, standing next to the food vendor carts, watching the passing parade of people along the street. After a few minutes, a scruffy homeless man, wearing a Vietnam War Veteran cap and a camouflage jacket, limped his way toward them. It was obvious that he had been wounded during the war. Queenie wondered if he had fallen on hard times or if he were a struggling addict who was unable, or maybe even unwilling, to find a job. Whatever the reason for his homelessness, she didn't care. All she cared about was the fact that he looked extremely hungry.

Just as he was about to pass by, she reached out and handed him the rest of her hot pretzel. He took it and finished it off happily, thanking her repeatedly as he went on his way.

Queenie nodded in his direction. "Think that guy was wondering where his next meal was coming from when he was crossing the street?"

"If he was, you just gave him his answer," said JJ.

Later that afternoon, Queenie and Pudge were busy strolling through the center of Faneuil Hall Marketplace, this time without the devious intent of swiping any tip jars. The air was cool and crisp, and Pudge shivered in the breeze.

"Why don't we get you a jacket," Queenie suggested, tugging on the hood of Pudge's shabby gray Nike sweatshirt. They walked past the famous Cheers restaurant and over the cobblestone road, weaving their way slowly through the afternoon crowd of shoppers, locals and tourists. The cross-eyed juggler was there this time, and they watched him briefly as he entertained a small circle of onlookers.

"Why do you always want to buy me something?" Pudge asked.

"I don't *always* want to buy you something," Queenie argued. "It's a simple case of have versus have not. I noticed that you've been wearing that same ratty sweatshirt for weeks now, and that you don't *have* a jacket. So I thought I'd get you one, because I *have* the means."

"But isn't that what Izzy gave you a hard time about, trying to help me with money?"

"Have I tried to buy you anything since the cheeseburger?" Queenie asked defensively. "In fact, I haven't mentioned spending a single dime on you since we started hanging out. I'm not trying to help you with money. I just want to do something nice for a friend who could use a new winter jacket." She reached over and pretended to wipe something off Pudge's shoulder. "I think it's time you dropped that chip off your shoulder. It's starting to lose its charm."

Pudge cracked a smile. "I know I can come off as snotty and tough, but I don't mean to be that way. Most of the kids on the street and at the shelter act that way, like my friend Sam. He's a really nice guy when you get to know him, but he's really angry with his parents right now, so that's why he was a little mean to you when you first met him. He's not like that all the time."

"It's one thing to act tough," said Queenie. "But keeping your guard up all the time keeps people who want to be your friend at arm's length."

"Yeah, but as long as I keep my guard up, it keeps me from getting attached to people and getting hurt when they don't follow through with their promises."

"That's quite an intellectual response from a fourteen-year-old."

"I'm just repeating what one of the counselors at the shelter told me. But I get what she's saying. My first instinct is to push people away, since my parents pushed me away. I'm just sick of being let down all of the time by people I trust."

Queenie couldn't argue with that. "I know it's hard for you to trust people right now and I want you to be able to trust me. But I don't want to push you into it, either. I know it's got to be on your own terms. When you're ready to let me in, let me know. And we'll go get you that new jacket."

"I can see why Izzy likes you so much," Pudge said after a moment.

Queenie came to halt. "Wait, she said that? She said that she likes me?"

"Well, not exactly. She used the word 'intriguing.' "

"She thinks I'm intriguing?" Queenie smoothed out the sleeves of her white Polo shirt, which she wore under her brown vest jacket. "And all this time I thought she couldn't stand me."

"So, I was right?" Pudge asked boldly. "You like her?"

"Let's just say that I find Miss Izzy alluring," Queenie grinned. "She's got this energy about her that's incredibly intoxicating. I can't put my finger on it. I'm used to saying a few charming things here and there and winning girls over instantly. But Izzy is different. She won't give me an inch. I've never met a girl like that before. It bothers me that she thinks I'm some egotistical rich girl who buys her way out of trouble. I mean, she may have been right at first. I used to be like that. But I'm changing. People are allowed to change, aren't they?" Queenie looked over at Pudge, who was wide-eyed with amusement.

"You do realize that you've just spent the last five minutes mumbling about Izzy, don't you?"

"No," Queenie replied blandly. "I didn't realize. But thanks for pointing it out."

"If it makes you feel any better, I think you two would make a cute couple."

"I appreciate that. But don't say anything to her about it. The only people who know that I am interested in Izzy are you and JJ, and I'd prefer to keep it that way."

They passed by a few clothing stores, distractedly gazing at the window displays.

"Does that mean you consider me a close friend," Pudge finally asked. "Because you shared a secret with me?"

"I consider you more than a friend," said Queenie, placing her hand on Pudge's shoulder. "I consider you my long lost little sister."

Pudge sighed. "I have a secret for you, too," she said. "I've never told anyone this before, not even Izzy. But what I missed most about not being home this summer is the Saturday afternoons my father and I would spend together at the pond in Jamaica Plain."

"As in, Jamaica?"

"No, silly. As in, Jamaica Plain, right here in Boston. There's a huge pond and park there. We'd rent a canoe and paddle around the pond for a little while. Then we'd go for ice cream afterwards. I miss that."

Pudge paused in front of Urban Outfitters. There, sitting comfortably in the window, was a manikin wearing a burnt orange jacket with thick sleeves and plenty of insulation.

"I miss the feeling I used to have of not having anything to worry about," she said, her eyes fixed on the jacket, "except what kind of ice cream I was going to get."

Queenie stood next to her in silence, not sure what to say.

"I don't know why I told you that," Pudge said after a moment. "I've just been missing home a lot lately."

"Hey, anytime you need to talk about it, I'm here for you."

Pudge nodded. Then she squished her finger against the windowpane. "You know, I think I might be ready for a jacket now."

Queenie smiled, rubbing her hands together. "Good," she said. "It's about time."

CHAPTER 13

"Did you get the flowers I sent?" JJ asked, once Kendal answered the phone. She was sprawled out on top of her unmade bed, wearing a pair of orange plaid, extra-large boxer shorts and a green T-shirt, taking a break from her homework.

"I did," said Kendal. "They were unexpected."

"I wanted to apologize for the way I was acting while you were here. I let my insecurities get the best of me, and instead of just enjoying your company, I acted like a complete moron."

"You didn't have to buy me flowers to apologize," said Kendal. "But I appreciate the gesture."

"There's something else that I have to tell you," said JJ. She cringed as she spoke into the phone, "To be honest, from the moment we climbed into the cab after you arrived, I felt like you were hiding something from me."

"You could have just told me that at the time."

"I know."

"Besides, I wasn't hiding anything from you. I think you were just picking up on the obvious—we aren't the same people as we were at Sampson."

"I know that, too," JJ said as she rolled over on her back and gazed upwards. She noticed a spider crawling slowly across the ceiling, each step precise and carefully placed. "I think we are both moving at our own pace," she said, focusing on the spider. "Instead of trying to keep pace with you, I should be supporting you. After all, you're my best friend."

"Queenie might have something to say about that," said Kendal.

"Queenie understands the difference," JJ replied. "And if she doesn't, she will soon enough. She's met someone that she likes a lot."

"Really? I thought Queenie would be a bachelorette for life."

"So did I. But I think she's met her match with this one. Most girls fall pathetically into Queenie's arms the moment she flashes a smile or says something witty. But this girl is different, and it's driving Queenie crazy."

"This girl sounds like she's someone I'd get along with. Maybe next time I come up to visit, you can introduce me to her?"

JJ smiled at the thought, even though she knew it wasn't going to happen. "I've been doing some thinking about that," she said. "About us visiting one another."

"You have?"

"Yeah, I have." JJ sucked in a quick breath. "I think we should take a break from visiting for a little while. Actually, I think we should just take a break in general."

After the outcome of their last visit, Kendal wasn't the least bit surprised. "Are you sure you want to do that?" she asked.

"Yes. I know that's what you really want right now. And it's probably for the best. I mean, I know that's what I need right now, too."

"JJ, I—"

"You don't have to tread lightly with me anymore," JJ interrupted. "I'm a big girl. I'm in college now, remember? I'll be fine. I'd rather do this willingly instead of clinging to you like a lost child. You're right about everything, Kendal. Last year was really special for us, and I'll always cherish the way we got together. But I agree that we should just let things go and see what happens."

"That's the beauty of our situation," said Kendal. "You

never know what's going to happen. What's that saying? If you love something, let it go. And if it comes back to you then it was meant to be?"

"Exactly. We may change our minds next month, or maybe next year, and try again. Or maybe, we'll end up as good friends. Either way, I'll always love you."

"I'll always love you, too," Kendal returned, affectionately. They sat quietly on the phone for a few minutes, since there wasn't much else to say.

"Listen," Kendal said at last. "I really hate to do this, but I've got to run. I'm late for a study group."

JJ recalled the days she used to tutor Kendal in the Page Library at Sampson Academy for her women's studies class. That was how they had met, and everything else had sprung from there. It felt so long ago, but JJ still remembered how nervous she felt the first time they were sitting face to face, and how the connection between them grew stronger every time they saw each other after that. "I want you to know that I'll always be here for you, no matter what happens with us," she said, feeling the need to make it clear.

"I know," said Kendal. Her voice squeaked and wavered a bit before she regained her composure. "I feel the same way."

As soon as she hung up the phone, JJ rolled back over on her stomach and pulled out her notebook. The clouds of her writer's block had begun to part, and in that moment she knew exactly what to write. Her pen hit the page feverishly. She filled ten pages then decided to switch over to her laptop and continue. Finally, when she could no longer keep her eyes open, JJ set the laptop aside and fell into her pillow knowing that as soon as she woke up in the morning, she'd be ready to write some more.

* * *

"What's the project for?" Pudge asked. "And why do you need my help?"

She was wearing her brand new burnt-orange jacket, even though they were eating breakfast in the shelter's warm and comfortable dining area. In fact, she hadn't taken off the jacket since the day Queenie bought it for her.

"It's for my sociology class," said Queenie over a cup of bland coffee and a plate of powdered eggs, dry toast and stringy bacon. "See, we're supposed to research a sociological issue and present it in front of the whole class. And after my experience with you and the shelter, I decided to focus on LGBT teen homelessness. I really want to do well on it and get my point across. You can help me with that. I'll do all of the grunt work, research and other boring stuff. All you need to do is tell your story during my presentation. That's it. With you presenting with me, I'm guaranteed to get an A."

Pudge grew silent. She glared at her plate of uneaten eggs and toast. "I knew it," she mumbled.

"Knew what?"

"I knew you were only being nice to me for a reason. And now I see why. You don't want to be my friend. You just want to use me to get a good grade in your dumb class." Pudge pushed her plate away. "You can have your jacket back. I don't want it anymore. She took off the jacket and threw it at Queenie, and then ran from the dining room.

Queenie was still sitting there wide-eyed and speechless, trying to figure out what had just happened when Izzy walked over.

"What was that about?" she asked, in an accusatory tone.

"I have no idea," Queenie said earnestly. "One minute I was explaining my sociology project to her, and the next

Lyndsey D'Arcangelo

minute she was throwing her new jacket in my face."

"What sociology project?"

"Well, since I started volunteering, my sociology professor assigned a project for class. He wants us to research a sociological issue and present it during class. You said yourself that there needs to be awareness about LGBT teen homelessness, so I thought I'd present on that. I figured Pudge could help me out by telling her story during the presentation, you know, in order to give it a personal edge. But I don't think she likes the idea all that much because she threw the jacket I just bought for her right at my face before storming off."

"It's obvious she thinks you were bribing her," Izzy said. "In other words, she thinks you bought her the jacket so she'd help you with the project."

"But I wasn't bribing her. I bought her the jacket to help keep her warm. The project has nothing to do with that. I just thought it would be something fun for us to do together, and that it would give her an opportunity to share her story with others. She's got this thing where she feels like no one cares. But if she helped with the project, she'd see that a lot of people do care."

Izzy sat down at the table next to Queenie. "Look, I know that you have good intentions and I've seen how much time you've been spending at the shelter lately. It's obvious to me that you really care about Pudge. But you have to understand how hard it is for her to open up and trust people. She's always looking for an excuse to cut and run, because it's easier that way."

"I know that. But what am I supposed to do? I can't seem to win with that kid."

"It's not about winning," said Izzy. "It's about letting her know that you aren't just being her friend so you can get something out if it. She needs to know that you aren't going to stop coming to the shelter once the project is over, or when you graduate from college. She needs to know that she's got a friend in you for life."

"How do I prove that? The best I can do is to give her my word."

"Words are useless. Actions mean more. There's nothing you can say right now. Just don't disappear. Keeping coming around, so that she can see that you aren't going anywhere, and that you are here for the right reasons. I know Pudge. She'll give you another chance. Maybe she'll even help you with the project. But it has to be on her terms."

"I don't even care about her helping me with the project at this point," said Queenie. "I just want her to know I'm for real." She shook her head and bit her lip.

"What?" asked Izzy.

"It's ironic, that's all. I used to bribe people all the time to get what I wanted. Now I finally do something that's genuine and Pudge thinks it's a bribe." Queenie stood up and handed Izzy the jacket. "Can you hold on to this for me? Hang it up in your office so Pudge can see that I didn't take it back. I have to run to school, but I'll try to stop by later on this afternoon." She picked up her breakfast tray from the table and turned to walk away.

"Wait," said Izzy. She pulled at the zipper on the jacket, fumbling with it in her hands. "Pudge has really had an impact on you, hasn't she?"

"Yeah," said Queenie. "She really has."

"I'm glad," said Izzy. Then she hesitated and added, "Are you busy tonight?"

"Not that I know of, why?"

"There's this documentary playing at a theater in Harvard Square that I've wanted to see. Would you like to come with me?"

"Wait a minute—are *you* asking me out?"

"No," Izzy maintained. "I'm asking if you want to come to a movie with me. As friends."

"That's a relief," Queenie said, playfully pretending to wipe sweat from her forehead. "For a minute there I thought you wanted to go on a date with me, or something."

Izzy smiled. "You would think that, wouldn't you?"

"You know me," said Queenie. "I'm all 'full of myself' and stuff."

"Just meet me in my office around eight, okay?"

"Okay. Sounds like a plan."

Izzy slid the jacket over her shoulder and stood up from the table. "And don't worry so much about Pudge. You've been amazing with her. She's just in a vulnerable place right now. You have to be patient, that's all. She'll come around."

"I hope so," Queenie replied. "I'm not planning on going anywhere, so she'll have to let her guard down with me eventually."

"She will," said Izzy. "You have a certain way with people."

"What do you mean?"

"You just have a way about you that makes people feel at ease and safe. That's why Pudge feels so comfortable around you."

"How do you know?"

"Because, it's the same reason why I feel so comfortable around you."

"Really?" Queenie asked, cocking an eyebrow. "Now I'm really curious. I thought you couldn't stand to be around me."

"I'm a lot like Pudge," Izzy confessed. "I tend to keep my guard up until I feel safe and comfortable enough to let someone in. I've been trying my hardest to keep my guard up around you. But there's something about you, Queenie."

"Pudge did tell me that you think I'm 'intriguing.' "

"She did, did she?"

"Is it true?"

"About as true as you thinking I'm 'alluring.'"

Queenie smirked. "Pudge is sure lousy at keeping secrets."

"She sure is," said Izzy. She swung her hips and spun around, letting the jacket drape over her shoulder. Right before she crossed the threshold of the doorway, she peeked at Queenie over her shoulder. As soon as their eyes locked, she smiled knowingly, and kept on walking.

CHAPTER 14

Queenie walked to her apartment late in the evening and found JJ sitting on the floor, next to a plate with a half-eaten sub and potato chips. There were endless scraps of notebook paper scattered about. JJ, cross-legged in front of her laptop, was pounding away at the keys, still dressed in her pajamas from the night before.

"Did you go to class today?" Queenie asked, making a pit stop in the kitchen for a glass of milk.

"I took a mental health day," JJ replied, without looking away from the computer screen.

"Is everything okay?" Queenie asked, as she walked back into the room and carefully assessed the situation. "Have we switched places or something? Is this a case of *Freaky Friday*?" She patted herself down. "I feel like I'm in the right body and everything."

"What are you talking about?" JJ asked, and sat back from her computer. She hadn't showered all day, and the dark circles under her eyes were clearly visible.

"What am I talking about? Have you looked in the mirror lately? You don't look so good, JJ. A month ago I was sitting where you are now, only without a laptop. Don't you remember? I was miserable, in a funk, at rock bottom. You basically were up, and I was down. Now, it's quite obvious to me that you are down, and I am up."

"*Really?*" said JJ.

"Look at the facts," said Queenie. She set the glass of milk down on the coffee table and held up her fingers. "I used to spend all day in my pajamas and skip class. Now you are the one skipping classes and spending all day in your pajamas. It's quite clear to me that we've switched places."

"I know how this looks," said JJ as she held up her hands. "But it's not what you think. I'm not depressed and I'm not in a funk. In fact, I'm flying high. I finally broke through my writer's block. I've been writing practically all night and all day. It just hit me out of nowhere. I can't stop."

"How long are you going to keep writing?"

"Until the motivation goes away, I guess."

Queenie picked up her glass of milk and drained it. She watched JJ for a minute in silence. "What you are writing about?"

"I'll explain later," said JJ. She was staring intently at the computer screen again. "It has a lot to do with Kendal, Sampson Academy, you, and—"

"Me?"

"Face it, Queenie. You make a great character."

"Yeah, I suppose I do. Anyway, I'll let you get back to it. I've got to get over to the shelter." She pretended to polish her nails against her jeans, and then examined them. "I've got a date with Izzy."

JJ's head shot up from her laptop. "You asked her out, and she actually said yes?"

"Actually, she asked *me* out."

"Shut up."

"Well, she sort of asked me out. She asked me to go see some documentary with her, as friends."

"At least she's making time for you. You must be growing on her, after all."

"I certainly hope so."

JJ leaned back and rested her hands on the floor behind her. "You really like her, don't you?"

"Yeah, I do. I can't help it. She's not like any other girl I've ever met. She's real. I've already told her things I wouldn't tell anybody, aside from you."

"It's about time you met someone like that. Most of the girls you've been with were train wrecks."

Queenie didn't argue. Instead, she set her empty glass back down on the coffee table. "How are things going for you? You know, with Kendal?"

JJ debated telling her that they had already broken up, but she wasn't prepared to talk about it, not yet anyway. "Let's say that I haven't changed my relationship status on Facebook to single just yet," she said instead.

"That's promising," said Queenie. "Nothing is ever official until you see it on Facebook."

JJ sighed. "But I still feel like Kendal is ready to let go and she's just hanging on because she doesn't want to hurt me. It isn't fair to her or to me. I've been thinking a lot about what you said the other day, and I'm trying to make sense of it all."

"I know it must be hard for you," said Queenie. "Kendal was everything to you."

"She 'was' everything and that's the problem. It's past tense. Things are different now. We're all different."

Queenie nodded in agreement then looked up at the wall clock. "I need to get going. I don't want to keep Izzy waiting, even if we are just hanging out as friends." She patted JJ lightly on the head. "I'll be home later if you want to talk some more."

"Thanks," said JJ. "But I'm okay. This is something I have to figure out on my own."

"Don't write too hard," Queenie called out as she headed for the front door.

"Only if you don't flirt too hard."

"I'll try my best, but I make no guarantees."

* * *

"We have to cancel our movie date," Izzy said frantically as soon as Queenie arrived at her office door.

"I thought it wasn't a date?" Queenie teased.

"I'm serious," said Izzy. She sat at her desk gripping the phone in front of her with a frightened look on her face.

"Why? What happened? Are you okay?"

"It's has nothing to do with me. It has to do with Pudge. She hasn't been back to the shelter since she stormed off this morning. No one has seen her, not even the kids she normally hangs out with. No one knows where she is." She picked up the phone, paused and set the receiver back down in frustration. "I don't know who I can call to help look for her."

"What about the police?"

Izzy pulled at her fingers. "I would call the police, but only as a last resort. They'd take her to the police station and call her parents. Then child protective services would have to get involved. Pudge has already said that she doesn't want to go into a group home or foster care."

"Can't you force her to go, especially if it's in her best interest?" Queenie asked.

"Since she is under eighteen, yes, child protective services can legally step in. But this is a special case because we don't really know what's going on with her parents. I know Pudge. If she were put into a group home or foster care, she'd only run away as soon as she got the chance. And if I call the police on her, I know she would never trust me again. Who knows where she'd go then? She might disappear, and we'd never see or hear from her again. It's happened before."

"I thought that this was normal, her coming and going as she pleased."

"In the summertime, yes. But that's because it warm enough to sleep on the streets or on park benches, or wherever. She's been here every night since it started getting colder out. I have a really bad feeling about this."

"Did anyone check the bus station?" Queenie asked.

"I sent someone over there already. But I doubt she had any money to purchase a ticket."

"She has to be somewhere," said Queenie. "I'm going to look for her myself."

"Where?"

"I don't know. I guess I'll just start with the place where we first met."

"Wait," said Izzy, as she reached for a red fleece jacket from the back of her chair. "I'll go with you."

They left the shelter and hailed a cab as soon as they reached the sidewalk. But after twenty minutes of bumper-to-bumper traffic, Queenie told the cab driver to let them off at the next block.

"We can get there faster if we just walk," she told Izzy. They left the cab and headed down the sidewalk, dodging people along the way. When they arrived at the familiar spot where she had first met Pudge, Queenie looked across the street. Burger King was still standing in the same exact place it was before. But Pudge was nowhere in sight.

Queenie paced around the empty street corner in defeat. "She's not here."

"Can you think of any other place she might be?" asked Izzy.

Queenie bent down in frustration, resting her hands on her knees.

"Think," Izzy pleaded. "Is there any place she may have mentioned when you were hanging out together?"

"I'm thinking as hard as I can," said Queenie. Then her eyes widened. "Wait! I remember her telling me about a spot she used to go with her father. I bet that's where she is."

They hurried around the corner and darted down the steps of the nearest subway station.

"This whole thing is all my fault," said Queenie, as they boarded the subway train and sat down. "I shouldn't have tried to get her to go along with my project. It was too soon. She had just started to open up to me."

"It's not your fault," Izzy protested. She zipped up her jacket. "You've been a good friend to her. Pudge is just really struggling right now. Being rejected by your own family is incredibly hard, and she's constantly putting up walls as a result. I should know, because I do the exact same thing."

"I keep thinking that this whole situation is going to work itself out, you know," said Queenie. "That Pudge's parents will come around, and welcome her back home like it's just a bad dream or something. I never thought she'd have to spend her entire adolescent life this way. But the more time I spend at the shelter, I see how naïve I really am. How can parents just turn their backs on their own kids for something they have no control over?"

Izzy reached over and placed her hand on Queenie's knee. "It's something that even I don't understand and I've lived through it. But that's why it's so important to get the word out. It's a harsh reality for many kids like Pudge. When your family turns their back on you, where else can you go for help?"

They sat quietly for a little while, until Izzy finally asked where they were going.

"Jamaica Plain," said Queenie. "There's a pond and a park there that Pudge used to go to with her father. She told me they would rent a canoe and paddle around the pond, then stop someplace for ice cream afterwards on their way home."

"She told you that?"

"Yeah, she did. I didn't even ask, you know? She was

beginning to open up to me. That's why I was so upset when she got angry with me this morning. I felt like I was making a real connection with her because she had started to let her guard down. Maybe this whole sociology project idea was a huge mistake."

"It's not a mistake. I'll talk to her."

"Let's hope we can find her first."

The subway stop at Heath Street was the last stop on the green line, so Queenie and Izzy were forced to walk the rest of the way to Jamaica Pond. It was after 10 PM when they finally reached the shoreline. Queenie held onto Izzy's hand as she led the way through the footpaths that wound up and around the pond. Park benches lined the path, and numerous people were using them as beds for the night.

"Maybe we should just give up and call the police after all," Izzy suggested as they made their way down the footpath. "Even if Pudge is here, there's no way we are going to see her in the dark."

"Let's at least circle all the way around the pond," said Queenie. "I have a strong feeling that she's here." They came to another clearing where a few more people slept on park benches. Queenie left Izzy's side, approaching each bench guardedly. There, on the farthest bench from the water, she spied Pudge. The girl was curled on her side in a fetal position, with the hood of her favorite gray sweatshirt pulled up over her head.

Queenie inched her way over. "Mind if I sit down?"

Pudge raised her head, and frowned. "What are you doing here?" she asked.

"Looking for you. What were you planning on doing, sleeping out here all fall and winter?"

"If I have to."

"When it snows, you might freeze to death."

"Who cares?"

"I care," said Queenie.

"You care about your stupid class," said Pudge. "You don't care about me."

"Do you really think I'd be out here in the dark looking for you if I didn't care about you? What do I have to do to prove to you that I'm your friend? So I asked you for help with a project. Don't you know me well enough to know it's a good thing? I mean the more people who know about kids like you, the better. That's all."

Once she saw Queenie sit down, Izzy hurried over to the other side of the bench. "You gave everyone at the shelter quite a scare," she told Pudge. "What were you thinking?"

Pudge sat up so that Izzy had a place to sit down. "Yeah, right," she said. "I doubt anyone even noticed that I was gone." She kept her hood up and her hands stuffed in the pockets of her sweatshirt.

"That's not true," said Izzy. "There are a lot of people at the shelter who care about you, and we were all worried about you when you didn't come back after you left this morning."

"I don't care," said Pudge. "I'm not going back there."

"Then we'll sit here all night with you," said Queenie. "But this bench probably isn't that comfortable when you have to sleep on it with two other people."

"I hope you like to snuggle," Izzy added.

Pudge studied Queenie's face, and then Izzy's. She could tell from the look in their eyes that they were serious. "You two are crazy," she told them. "Don't you know how dangerous it is to be out here at night?"

"That's exactly why we came looking for you in the first place," said Izzy. "Come on. Let's go back to the shelter where it's safe and warm. It's cold, and really scary out here."

"It's not so bad," said Pudge, shivering in the darkness.

"I bet it would be better with a jacket," said Queenie as she pinched Pudge on the arm. "Maybe a bright burnt-orange jacket, with plenty of warm and cozy stuffing?"

Pudge struggled to keep from laughing. "Fine, I'll go back," she said, with a fake scowl. "But I'm still not helping you with your stupid project."

"Whatever you say," said Queenie. "Let's just get out of here."

CHAPTER 15

JJ sat in the seat nearest to the window, watching the bustling streets of Northampton slowly fade into the background as the bus drove away. She had decided to venture west of Boston that afternoon and headed for the small city known as NoHo, on a mission to tour the picturesque Smith College campus.

Smith College was a lot like Sampson Academy. It was built in the late 1800s and possessed a certain colonial charm. It was also a lot smaller than most colleges. For JJ, it was a clear reminder of everything she missed about a small private liberal arts school. It certainly beat getting swallowed up in the oversized and crowded classrooms at Boston University. With sometimes as many as a hundred students in a class, JJ felt as if she were just another name on the attendance sheet. She hadn't connected to any of her professors the way that she had hoped, and with Queenie so preoccupied lately, she found herself longing for a change of scenery. Boston was exciting and fun, yes. But over the course of the semester, it had lost its luster. JJ craved greenery, tall trees and nature, instead of the cars, concrete, and tall buildings she saw whenever she looked out her apartment window or stepped outside. Something was missing. And as soon as the bus had pulled into Northampton, JJ felt as though she'd found what she had been looking for. NoHo was a small city with a small town feel, and it even had a local corner coffee shop to prove it.

That was the first stop JJ made when she stepped off the bus. She had picked up a fresh cup of coffee, and sat at a corner table observing the diverse mix of patrons as they each wandered in to satisfy their coffee cravings. A bulletin board caught JJ's attention. It featured announcements of numerous poetry readings, writer's groups and local creative writing workshops. She scanned the board, finally pulling off a piece of paper with the number of a local writer's group, and picking up a flier announcing an open mic night. Then she crossed the street, and headed up the hill to the admissions office of Smith College. After the campus tour, she stopped in the English and literature building to speak to a professor she had been exchanging e-mails with about the possibility of a transfer. By the time she boarded the bus to head back to Boston, she was more than ready to enroll at Smith, and make the move to NoHo without a second thought.

There was one thing holding her back, however, and that was Queenie. JJ knew her friend wouldn't be thrilled about her decision to leave Boston University, especially since JJ had just convinced Queenie that Boston was the perfect place to be, in order to get Queenie out of her funk. It turned out that JJ had been right on one account. Boston *was* the perfect place—for Queenie. But it wasn't the perfect place for her. Not anymore. Whether she wanted to or not, sooner than later, she was going to have to tell Queenie the truth.

Queenie fought hard to keep her eyes open. She had been at the Boston University library, researching statistics and reviewing information on LGBT teen homelessness, since dinnertime.

At Sampson Academy, she had only stepped inside the library a handful of times, and that was usually because she had been looking for JJ. It was like a foreign country to her, and she needed time to explore it in order to learn her way around.

Queenie sneaked in an extended yawn, and rubbed the small of her back. School had always come easy to her, thanks to her photographic memory and the innate ability to soak up information, when she actually paid attention in class. But if she was going to get an A on her sociology project and do well in college, then she was going to have to buckle down and study—and that meant spending lots of time in the library.

The recent incident with Pudge had certainly made a profound impact on Queenie. She even had called her parents the next day to tell them how much she loved them, and that she was sorry for taking advantage of them in the past. They were caught completely off guard, and didn't really understand why Queenie was calling to apologize. She had never done so before, and to tell her parents that she loved them was a rare occurrence. But after seeing Pudge sleeping on a park bench in the dark, all alone, something had shifted inside of Queenie. She suddenly realized how lucky she was to have parents who accepted and loved her, despite everything she had put them through. All of the obscene credit card bills she had racked up, the snotty remarks and rebellious acts that she committed, had been her way of getting back at her parents. But just what she was getting back at them for, she couldn't quite figure out. They accepted the fact that she wasn't interested in being a socialite, that she was willing to carve out her own name for herself, and that she was gay. They never tried to change her, or disown her. They loved her regardless, even if they had to get used to the idea that she was different from what they had expected. And she had been taking their love for granted because she couldn't accept them for who they were. The phone call home was Queenie's way of starting over. She was more convinced now then ever that it was time to make changes, and she had Pudge to thank for that.

"There you are," Queenie heard from over her shoulder. She turned around to see JJ standing in front of a row of books, dangling two cups of Dunkin Donuts coffee in the air.

"Hooray for reinforcements!" Queenie sang as she bent forward and stretched her back. Then she muttered less enthusiastically, "How do people like you do this all the time?"

"Do what?"

"Study. It takes so much time and energy. I've only been here for a few hours, but I feel like I've been here for days."

"Welcome to the wonderful world of the average college student." JJ pulled up a chair beside the table and handed her a cup of coffee. "Finding any good information for your project?"

"Actually, yes. Did you know that, according to Parents and Friends of Lesbians and Gays, forty percent of homeless youth identify themselves as gay, lesbian or bisexual? Forty percent!"

"That's a lot."

"And get this, approximately twenty-eight percent of gay teens drop out of high school because of excessive bullying and discomfort. That's insane."

"Not really. You know how things were in high school. We may not have gotten bullied at Sampson but we were definitely treated differently by some people, just because they knew we were gay. Some kids get it even worse. For your next project, you should tackle bullying."

"Maybe. I never really put much thought into all this stuff before, because we never had to deal with it. But now that I'm actually sitting here looking at it, it's kind of in my face."

"That's what the library is here for, my friend. Books and

books of information, waiting just for you."

"Who knew?" Queenie took a long sip from her cup. "At least I didn't get lost like I did the past couple of times I came to the library. I was wandering around the rare books section for at least twenty minutes."

JJ laughed. "I'll wait for you. That way you won't get lost on the way out. When are you going to call it quits?"

"In another hour or so, I hope."

"You must really enjoy what you're working on. I've never seen you put this much time and effort into a school-related project before."

"I've never had a school project that I cared so much about. Meeting Pudge was the best thing that could have happened to me. It really opened my eyes to other things."

"Like what?"

"Like the fact that I've been a jerk to my parents for the better part of my teenage years, for stupid and selfish reasons. Even though they had to get used to the idea of having a gay daughter, they never would have stopped loving me for being gay, or cut me off. Pudge's situation helped me realize how fortunate I am to have them as my parents, even if we don't always see eye to eye. I used to throw my sexuality in their faces for no good reason."

"I never understood why you were so hard on them all the time. But I'm glad you finally realize it. You've definitely changed, Queenie. You haven't even tried to drag me out of the apartment for a night out in weeks."

"It's been quite a long time since I've been out myself," said Queenie. "I don't miss it, though. All of my free time is spent at the shelter and hanging around with Pudge. I know we haven't been able to hang out a lot lately, and I'm sorry about that. Our schedules don't match up so well, and when I'm not at the shelter, I'm usually here working on the project."

"It's okay," said JJ, staring down at her coffee cup. "I've

been busy, too. Spending time by myself has been good for me."

"How so?" asked Queenie.

"Oh, you know, just that I feel more independent and stuff." JJ longed to change the subject, because she wasn't yet ready to tell Queenie about Smith College. "How are things with Izzy?"

"I'm not really sure. Our plans to hang out the other night fell apart when Pudge ran away. We haven't seen each other since. I don't know what's going on or where I stand with her. I'm thinking of asking her out, but I'm waiting for the right time."

"Well, don't wait too long to ask. The fact that Kendal and I weren't able to spend time together is why we broke up."

Queenie spit up her coffee, and it dribbled down the front of her cream-colored zip-up sweater. "Wait, what?"

JJ looked on in amazement, and handed over a napkin. "Uh, you got a little coffee on your sweater."

Queenie ignored the napkin. "When did you break up with Kendal?"

"I wouldn't say that I broke up with her exactly. It was more of a mutual thing."

"Why didn't you tell me?"

"When it first happened, I wasn't ready to talk about it. I needed to sort through it all myself. I can't always depend on you to point me in the right direction. I need to start making decisions on my own."

"So, what did you decide?"

"I decided that Kendal needs time to explore New York, and have some fun in college without any restrictions. And I need some time to be by myself for a little while."

"Wow," Queenie said genuinely. She studied JJ for a moment. "You're not even freaking out or anything. You seem totally okay with it."

JJ hit Queenie lightly in the arm. "I am okay with it, silly. I know I used to get a little neurotic now and then, but I like to think I've grown up a bit. Besides, Kendal and I talked it through. It's not that we don't love each other—it's that we love each other enough to let go and see what happens."

Queenie still couldn't shake her disbelief. "But she was THE girl, THE one. You spent an entire semester at Sampson pining over her and figuring out how to win her over."

"Exactly. I've always put so much energy into making someone else happy that I ended up neglecting myself. It's time to find out what makes me happy, and who I really am. Remember that day at Boston Common when you asked me if I was scared to be alone?"

"Yeah, I think I recall saying something profound like that."

"I need to know that I'm okay being with myself, and that my happiness doesn't hinge on someone else. That's a lot of pressure to put on someone. And I care too much about Kendal to put her in a position like that. If she and I are really meant to be together, it will happen."

"And if you're not meant to be together?"

"Then, it's like you said—we'll always have Sampson."

Queenie nodded in agreement, and then noticed a thick red binder sitting on the table. "Is that yours?"

"Yeah. I figured I'd do a little work while I was here. I haven't been spending as much time in the library as I probably should."

"What is it?"

"It's something I'm working on for my creative writing class."

"It looks big."

"It is—in both the literal and metaphorical sense."

Queenie picked up the binder and examined it. "What is it, exactly?"

"It's my first novel, I'm proud to say." JJ said. "It's the

reason why I've been writing so much lately. The grade I get on this particular project is going to be my final grade for the semester. My professor is giving me a break, since I had a bad case of writer's block, and kept getting bad grades on every writing assignment I handed in. She knew I was trying really hard and putting the work in, so she took pity on me. When I got the idea for this novel," JJ carefully retrieved the binder from Queenie's hands, "I showed it to her and she was impressed. She said if I could finish it by the end of the semester, she'd grade me on it instead of everything else I've been turning in. It's my 'redeemer' shot."

"Redeemer shot? Oh, you mean like in the game P.I.G.?"

"Right. I have all three letters and I've got one foul shot to stay alive in the game."

"Uh, good luck with that," said Queenie, turning back to her books.

"What's that supposed to mean?"

"You were never all that good at P.I.G."

"Gee, thanks for the support."

"I'm just playing with you," Queenie laughed. "You're a great writer. You have nothing to worry about. When do you have to have it done?"

"It's due when we get back from Thanksgiving break."

"That's when my project is due, too."

"Then I guess we should both get back to work," said JJ.

CHAPTER 16

Izzy sat with her back facing her office door as she emptied out some old files from her desk. She caught a whiff of a familiar scent, and felt a pair of hands gently cover her eyes.

"I've been wondering what you've been up to," Izzy said, without removing the hands.

Queenie spun Izzy's chair around, "How did you know it was me?"

"Just a hunch," said Izzy. "Where have you been hiding?"

"In the library. It's this large building with lots of books, tables and computers. And in those books, there's lots of useful information. I had no idea such a thing existed."

Izzy laughed. "I've missed your little jokes."

"I've missed the sound of your laughter." Queenie hesitated, took a deep breath, and then continued. "Maybe we can try planning another movie night since the last one ended the moment Pudge decided to journey off to Jamaica Plain."

"I'd like that," said Izzy. "I thought maybe you disappeared."

"You still don't have any faith in me, do you?"

"No, it's not that. This whole situation with Pudge is a delicate one. And, with everything that's happened, I would have understood if it was too much for you to handle. Spending time with her is one thing, but going out at night to look for her is another. Something very unpleasant could have happened to either of us."

"But nothing happened. And if I hadn't spent so much

time with her in the first place, she wouldn't have told me that story about her dad, and we wouldn't have found her when we did." Queenie leaned against Izzy's desk. "Everything happens for a reason. Besides, that whole incident just made me more determined than ever to finish this project and get the word out. So I'm moving forward without Pudge's help."

"Have you asked her about it again?" asked Izzy.

"Nope. And I don't plan on it, either. I'm back on her good side, and I want to keep it that way."

"Maybe you should try a different approach? I know that she looks up to you, Queenie. I think that if you presented it in another way, she'll jump at the chance to help you. "

"You think so?"

Izzy nodded her head gently.

"Okay, then. I'll take your advice." Queenie held her hands up in the air, "I guess we'll see what happens."

Pudge leaned over to get a good look at the screen of Queenie's laptop computer and at the rest of the papers that were spread out on the table in front of her, but Queenie shifted her lanky body and easily blocked her view.

"How come you won't let me see what you're doing?" she asked.

"Because you said you weren't interested."

"But lately all you do is work on that project. Won't you at least tell me what it's about?"

Queenie stopped typing and looked up. "I told you before, it's for a class at school, and it's important to me. You said that you didn't want anything to do with it, so I won't bore you with the details."

"I kind of want to know what it's about."

Queenie began typing again. "I thought you weren't interested?"

"Maybe I changed my mind," said Pudge. With a slight frown she muttered, "It's boring to sit here watching you work on it all the time. Maybe I can help?"

"Didn't you tell me loud and clear the other night that you weren't going to help me with my 'stupid' project?"

Pudge stared at her for a moment then looked down at the table. "I was just upset. I didn't really mean it."

"It doesn't matter to me if you help or not," said Queenie. "I still have to get it done for class. There are no chains or ropes attached to you, so you don't have to sit here and watch me work on this if you don't want to. You can go do something else."

Pudge pulled at a loose thread on her sweatshirt. "I don't want to do something else. I want to hang out with you."

Queenie manufactured a heavy sigh. "Just so you know, I'm going to be working on this project a lot over the next couple of weeks. That means that I might have to do some work while I'm here at the shelter."

"I know."

"But if you're really interested in what I'm working on, I'll gladly tell you more about it."

"I'm interested," Pudge maintained. She lifted a piece of paper from the pile and studied it for a moment. Then she looked at the chart and photographs on Queenie's laptop screen. "What's that chart there for, and who are those kids?"

Queenie closed the laptop and turned to face Pudge. "Did you know that nationally LGBT teens make up approximately forty percent of homeless kids in cities? Or that twenty-seven percent of LGBT teens have moved out or run away from home at least once because of arguments with family members about their sexual orientation?"

"Wow, I didn't know that. But I bet I could have guessed.

Most of my street friends are gay, so it's probably even more."

"There are kids like you and your friends all over the country," said Queenie. "That's the reason why I wanted you to help me with the project, so you could see that you're not the only one going through this. You can even come to the library and help me look up stuff. I promise I won't include you in the project unless you want to be involved. Just having you work on it with me is good enough."

"How were you going to include me in the project?" Pudge asked, suddenly intrigued.

"It's one thing to read statistics and look at photos and videos and all that. But it's another thing completely to have a real homeless gay teen standing in front of you, telling you 'this is my life because my parents don't accept me.' I'd have you stand up in front of the class and tell your story, to demonstrate the reality of LGBT teen homelessness. That's basically it."

"Why would anyone want to listen to what I have to say?" Pudge asked. "I'm just some dumb kid off the streets."

"You aren't just some dumb kid off the streets, Pudge. You're amazing. You've got more courage than anyone else I've ever met. Your story is the same as so many other kids who are going through the same thing. You'd be taking a negative situation and using it to bring about positive change. Why wouldn't they listen to what you have to say?"

"Do you really think it will help make a difference?"

"Yeah, I do."

Pudge played with the loose thread on her sweatshirt once more. "Izzy told me the other day that I'm too hard on you."

"She did?"

"She also said that I haven't given you the benefit of the doubt even though you did the same for me. She's right. I've been kind of a jerk to you, when all you've been trying to do is be my friend. And you've been a good friend to me, just like you said you were going to be. I want to pay you back, so yes, I'll do it. I'll help you with your project."

"Don't do it to repay me," said Queenie. "Do it because you want to."

"I do want to," Pudge declared. "I want to do it for you, and also for myself. It's like you said, I want something positive to come out of this." She grinned, and continued, "It's probably better that I spend time helping you with a school project than stealing tip jars, anyway."

Queenie pointed at her. "You got that right. I'm not getting arrested for you ever again. That's a promise."

"So, what do you need me to do?"

"I need to head over to the school library to go over a bunch of statistics. Why don't you come with me? Then I'll take you to meet my professor so we can get moving on the rest of the project."

"Okay," said Pudge. She stood up excitedly. "Let's do this thing."

CHAPTER 17

"Nice tie," Pudge snorted, as soon as she shook Professor Duncan's hand.

He looked down at the purple and green checkered tie around his neck, and let out a kind of low 'hrrmph.'

"She doesn't mince words," Queenie explained, as she placed her hands on Pudge's shoulders. "Believe it or not, it's part of her charm."

"Evidently," said Professor Duncan. He welcomed both Queenie and Pudge into his office, and offered them chairs in front of his desk. "What brings you two ladies to my office on this fine October afternoon?"

"We were in the library working on my project," Queenie explained. "And I thought I'd bring Pudge over to meet you."

"Queenie has told me a lot about you," Professor Duncan said to Pudge. "I think you're very brave for putting yourself out there and helping her with her project."

Pudge rolled her shoulders back confidently, "It's no big deal."

"Well, actually it is a big deal," Professor Duncan replied. He adjusted his tie and sat back in his desk chair. "You'll be speaking in front of a class of about a hundred students. And, if all goes well, I'd like you and Queenie to present your project to some of my other classes as well."

Pudge gasped. "A hundred students?"

"You'll be fine," Queenie said with a casual nod. "I'll be standing right next to you the entire time."

"But that's a lot of people."

"Exactly. The more people we can reach the better."

"Do you think you're up to this?" Professor Duncan asked.

"Uh, sure," Pudge stuttered, not wanting to let her nervousness show. "Of course I am."

"I understand that your family situation is very delicate at the moment," he pressed. "Maybe it's time we put our heads together and figure out a possible solution?"

Pudge's face quickly drained of color. She turned to Queenie in a panic. "Is this a set up? Are you planning on putting me in a group home or something?"

"No, that's not what he means at all," Queenie said, eyeing Professor Duncan. "Right?"

"Right," Professor Duncan reassured. "I wouldn't force you to do anything you don't want to do. But as the supervising adult in this particular situation, I feel that it's necessary to figure out a viable solution. You're just a child." He leaned forward. "And living on the streets is no way to grow up. Even if you don't want to go home, or can't go home, I think it's time to start thinking about some other options. Living in a group home or with a foster care family are possible options."

Pudge's eyes shifted to the floor. "I don't want to live with a foster care family," she said. "And I don't want to go to a group home, either."

Queenie forced an awkward cough. "Okay. I've been thinking about this for a while now, and I agree with Professor Duncan."

Pudge's head shot up. "You do?"

"I agree with the fact that you can't keep living on the streets. You've got to consider your future, Pudge. You've got to get back into school, get your diploma and help yourself. And you can't do that on the streets." She leaned over in her chair, and looked closely at Pudge. "I know you pretty well now and how hard it is for you to trust people. I don't think you'll be comfortable going to live with some weird family or living in a group home with a bunch of random kids that you don't even know. That's why I thought that you could live with me instead—if you felt comfortable enough."

Professor Duncan's eyes expanded. "Queenie, I . . . ."

"I know what you're going to say," she quickly interrupted and faced him head on. "But I've honestly thought this whole thing through."

"I don't think you have."

"Are you serious?" asked Pudge.

"Yes," said Queenie. "But I wouldn't want you to do it unless you felt comfortable, and only after you've talked with your parents to see if they'll let you come back home, first."

"Well, that part I agree with," said Professor Duncan.

"I know it's a huge step," Queenie said to him. "But I would only want to put Pudge in the best position possible to succeed. If she stays with me, she'll have a roof over her head, a warm bed to sleep in, and a welcoming place to call home." She turned back to Pudge. "I've read my fair share of statistics on this stuff lately, and if you stay on the street the outlook isn't good. I don't want you to become just another lost child statistic."

Professor Duncan rose from his chair and folded his hands behind his back as he walked around his office. "I will support you on one condition," he said firmly. "I want you to promise me that you'll bring a social worker with you and Pudge when you talk with her parents about her situation. A social worker can speak on Pudge's behalf and make sure she's properly protected."

"Okay," said Queenie.

"This is a serious situation, and something I wouldn't expect you to handle all by yourself. Like it or not, you're still just a budding college freshman."

"Is this something I have to do right now?" Pudge asked. "I'm not ready to go see my parents yet."

"No," said Professor Duncan. "But it has to happen sooner than later. It's time to get you off the streets, Pudge, whether that means moving back in with your family, or in with Queenie. She's right. We can't let you become just another statistic. We are in a position to help you, and that's what we are going to do."

* * *

JJ knew that Queenie wanted to talk to her about something important, since she was more cryptic than usual on the phone when she requested they meet at Newbury Street for a little shopping. Newbury Street is considered the Rodeo Drive or Fifth Avenue of Boston, which meant that Queenie was planning on spending some money. Queenie only ever went shopping when something serious was on her mind. Then she'd spend excessive amounts of her parents' money, instead of dealing with whatever was bothering her.

Instead of taking the train, JJ hopped on a bus for a little change of pace. Twenty minutes later she arrived at the far end of Newbury Street and met Queenie outside of the Patagonia store.

"Why didn't we just go to the outlet mall instead?" JJ asked. "Newbury Street is way too expensive."

"Did you suddenly forget that I'm a McBride, heiress to a Southern fortune beyond my wildest dreams? I have money to spend."

"I thought the days of abusing your parents' money were over?"

"As far as running up their credit cards, yes. But I still get a substantial monthly allowance, whether I ask for it or not.

I might as well put it to good use."

"What exactly are you shopping for?" JJ asked.

"I'm not sure. I guess it's more of a browsing day than a shopping day."

"Browsing?" JJ asked skeptically. "You hate browsing. And as far as shopping is concerned, you only go when something is bothering you. So spill it. What's up?"

"Nothing is up." Queenie smiled on cue. "I just wanted to spend some quality time with my best friend, that's all. I've been so busy lately, and I've missed hanging out with you."

"And now you're buttering me up," JJ observed. "Come on, Queenie. I've known you since our freshman year of high school. I can tell when you're hiding something, especially when you get the urge to spend large sums of money. It's your way of avoiding reality."

"All right," Queenie gave in. "You could have at least let me ease my way into it. Let's go grab some coffee."

"What happened to browsing?"

"You know how much I hate browsing." Queenie laughed and punched JJ gently in the shoulder with her fist.

They walked a few blocks down Newbury Street and entered a Starbucks. Queenie purchased two coffees while JJ found a table near the back of the room.

"I've been trying to figure out the right way to tell you this all day," said Queenie, sitting down across the table and sliding one of the cardboard cups over to JJ. "I'm not exactly sure how you're going to react."

"It can't be that bad," said JJ.

"It's not bad at all. It's actually something quite good."

"Then why are you worried about my reaction?"

"Because you get a little uptight about things now and again. And this is something that is going to directly affect you."

"Will you spit it out already?" JJ waved her hands into the

air, "You always build everything up as if it's earth-shattering news or something." She picked up her coffee, but it still was too hot to drink.

"Fine." Queenie took an extended sip from her cup. "I asked Pudge if she would like to live with us."

"You did what?" JJ nearly dropped her coffee.

"Look, she's a good kid. And she can't keep living on the streets any longer."

"Have you heard of a little government system called foster care?"

"She doesn't want to go into foster care, JJ. She'll only run away again. She said she would, and I believe her. And then what happens after that? It's hard for her to trust people. She doesn't even fully trust me yet, and we've spent a lot of time together. She has no one else to take her in. If she had a place to stay, she could go back to school and graduate like a regular kid."

"Queenie, we're practically still kids ourselves. What do we know about taking care of a teenager?"

"Pudge is smart enough to take care of herself. It's not like we'd have to baby her or anything. We're just providing a roof over her head, some food in her stomach, and some clothes on her back."

"Isn't there some legal steps you need to go through for something like this?"

"Just to have her stay with us? No. If I wanted to obtain legal guardianship, then that's completely different."

"Your parents are cool with this?"

"I haven't exactly told them yet," Queenie confessed. "But I plan on bringing Pudge home with me for Thanksgiving so they can get to know her better. I figure I can tell them about the situation before I get home." Queenie stared at JJ in silence. "You're not saying anything. You're not okay with this, are you?"

JJ pretended to be reading the writing on the side of her coffee cup. Finally she said, "I guess I'm okay with it, but I also have something to tell you." She slowly set the coffee cup down on the table. "I was going to wait until the end of the semester but maybe it's better to get it out now."

"What is it?"

"I'm going to transfer to Smith College. I start there in the spring."

Queenie's body swung forward in her seat. "What? Are you serious? Why?"

"We both know that I've been spending a lot of time by myself lately, and I've come to the conclusion that I'm not a city kind of girl. I followed you here, Queenie. Just like I followed you everywhere at Sampson Academy. But I need to start doing what's best for me. And I don't think living in Boston is it. I've already filled out the paperwork and talked to an admissions counselor at Smith. It's a great school, and they have smaller classes and a really good English and literature department. It's more my speed."

"I can't believe this," said Queenie. "You're totally bailing on me because of Pudge."

"Wait a minute," JJ argued. "That's not it at all. This doesn't even have anything to do with Pudge or your project. The truth is that I've been thinking about this for weeks now. I even went to Northhampton a few weekends ago to check out the campus and the area. You've been so preoccupied with your own life that you probably didn't even notice I was gone."

"That isn't fair. You know that I'm doing something I really care about for the first time in my life. I never knocked you when you spent more time with Kendal than you did with me last summer."

"The truth comes out," JJ snapped.

"What truth?"

"You've always been jealous about my relationship with Kendal."

Queenie pushed her chair back from the table. "That's ridiculous, and you know it." She stood up. "I'm leaving before one of us says something that we regret."

"I can't stick around in a place that wasn't right for me to begin with," JJ continued as she climbed out of her chair. "It has nothing to do with you, or Pudge or anything. Honest. It has everything to do with me. I hate stepping out of my front door and getting swallowed up by crowds of people. I hate the constant street noise outside my window, and the hurried pace of everything. This city is perfect for you, Queenie. I always knew that. But it's not for me. I followed you here because you're my best friend and that's what I've always done. But I can't keep following you the rest of my life. I have to start somewhere."

Queenie chewed on JJ's words and swallowed hard. "It's actually perfect timing," she said as she turned to leave. "Because you can start right here and now, by not following me out the door."

CHAPTER 18

Pudge rolled over on the cot, trying to get comfortable on the lumpy lopsided cushion beneath her. The common sleeping area at the shelter was shadowy and quiet, aside from a few coughs, sneezes and snores erupting sporadically from around the room. She pulled the blanket up over her shoulder to keep warm, and then threw it aside after getting too hot. She tried lying flat on her back for a few minutes, and when that didn't work she rolled over onto her stomach for a little while. It didn't really matter how Pudge positioned her body on the cot, because she couldn't stop the thought of reuniting with her parents from running through her mind.

"Pssst," she whispered into the darkness. "Sam, are you asleep?"

Sam stirred and moaned in the cot beside her. "I was," he grunted lazily. "What do you want?"

"Do you ever—do you think about going home again?"

"Why would I want to go home again? I've been back enough times already. It's obvious that my parents don't want anything to do with me, so I don't want to have anything to do with them. I'm fine right where I am."

"But don't you ever miss them?"

"Miss them? I miss the way they used to treat me before they found out I was gay. But I don't miss my father calling me a sissy because I don't like to play football. And I don't miss my stepmother telling me how I should act more masculine, and that something is wrong with me because I like boys. I don't miss any of that at all." He turned his body so that he was facing the opposite direction, and Pudge guessed he was done talking for the night.

She rolled over once more, recalling one snowy Christmas morning a couple of years ago. That Christmas, she had asked her parents for a new bicycle. Before sunrise, she awoke excitedly in her bed and leapt out onto the cold floor without giving a second thought to being quiet. She ran downstairs to the living room and grinned widely as soon as she spotted the brand new brightly-colored bicycle near the Christmas tree. It had a large red bow tied to the handlebars, and rested comfortably upright on its kickstand. She was so caught up in the moment that she didn't even hear her father come into the room behind her. He placed his large hands on her shoulders and kissed her lightly on the cheek.

"Merry Christmas, angel," he whispered.

Pudge felt the wetness of tears gathering in her eyes, as she remembered running to the bicycle and sitting on it in the middle of the living room. She didn't even care about any of the other gifts around the tree. The bicycle was the only gift she wanted. And her parents loved her enough to get it for her.

The memory quickly faded, and Pudge became aware once again of her current surroundings. This year, Christmas would be spent at the shelter. There wouldn't be a bicycle standing near the tree, she wouldn't have a nice wool quilt on her bed to keep her warm, and her father wouldn't be coming up behind her to kiss her on the cheek, and to say "Merry Christmas."

She didn't understand how things could have changed so drastically, simply by telling her parents the truth, that she was gay. One moment, her father called her an angel and the next he called her a disappointment. He abruptly took his love away and emphatically stated that homosexuality was unnatural, and that she was no longer his daughter. He couldn't understand why she would choose such a lifestyle.

But why would anyone choose to spend Christmas all alone in a homeless shelter when they could spend it in a warm home, surrounded by loving family, friends and relatives? If she did have a choice, Pudge knew that she would choose her family over anything else. But the decision had been made for her at birth. The truth was that she had no choice about her sexuality.

When she left home three months earlier, Pudge had hoped that her parents would welcome her back with open arms soon enough. But as of today, they still hadn't made any effort whatsoever to find her. She had stayed away because that is what she thought they wanted. But maybe it was time to go home again. Maybe once they saw her they would remember all those special moments, like that one Christmas morning with the bicycle, and forget about everything else. Maybe they just needed a little time to realize that, above all else, she was still their only child—gay or straight.

Pudge curled up in a tight little ball. She rubbed her eyes and yawned, wondering when she'd finally be able to fall asleep. There was one thing she knew for sure, however. It was time to go home and see her parents. She missed them and she wanted to know if they missed her just as much. Even though the thought made her extremely anxious, at least she didn't have to do it alone.

She closed her eyes and pictured Queenie in her mind. Most of her street friends didn't have anyone else to turn to. But she had Queenie. She had Izzy. Now, she even had Professor Duncan. She had plenty of people around her who cared about her, and who would do anything for her—even though they weren't family.

Pudge opened her eyes again.

She may not have a choice when it came to her sexuality, but she did have a choice when it came to her future. She could choose to keep living on the streets and keep feeling sorry for herself, or she could choose to be like Izzy, and rise above the situation. And if her father was unable to accept his own daughter for the person she really was, well then, that was his choice and he'd have to live with it.

Pudge only hoped that she would still feel as confident when she stood face to face with her parents.

* * *

That morning, the bicycle path that generously spread itself around the Charles River and wound its way up to Harvard Square and through Harvard University was particularly crowded. Queenie found herself weaving in and out of the way of runners, bikers and extreme walkers alike. She strolled along the river's edge, hoping for some clarity. But when she looked up and saw a familiar face approaching, her stressful thoughts dissipated into the chilled morning air, as if she had just spoken them aloud.

"Fancy meeting you here," Izzy said, hugging herself to keep warm. She was dressed in jeans, a mud-brown sweater and a plaid fall jacket. The mittens on her tiny hands matched the color of her sweater.

"Out for a relaxing morning stroll?" Queenie asked, her leather jacket zipped all the way up to the top and her bare hands stuffed deep down into the pockets of her jeans.

"Actually, yes," said Izzy. "Then I saw you coming from the opposite direction, so I thought I'd catch up and say hello."

"I'm glad that you did."

"I like your hat." Izzy pointed to the dark blue American Eagle skullcap on Queenie's head. "It suits you."

"Keeps my ears warm," said Queenie. As they began to

walk, she realized Izzy wasn't paying attention and yanked her out of the way of an oncoming biker.

"Whoa! That was close," Izzy said, dramatically pressing a hand to her chest. "I think you just saved my life."

Queenie forced a laugh, and kept walking.

"Is something wrong?" Izzy asked. "You're much more quiet than normal."

"Just your average quarrel with your best friend." Queenie inhaled the sweet scent of the river mixed with fallen leaves. "I love the fall, you know? I think it's my favorite time of year."

"I do, too." Izzy reached over touched Queenie's arm. "Hey, are you okay?"

"I don't know. I suddenly feel as though some big changes are on the horizon, and I'm not sure if I'm really ready for them." Queenie looked down at Izzy, who at 5"1' was much shorter than herself. "I don't know if you know this, but most of the time I like to act like I've got it all together when I really don't."

"I think I may have picked up on that."

"Is it that obvious?"

"No," said Izzy. "It's not. But I think I've gotten to know you well enough that I can tell when something is on your mind."

"That's an understatement," said Queenie. "First, JJ dropped a bomb on me, and told me that she wants to move to Northhampton and go to Smith College in the spring. Add that in with all the stress that's associated with the sociology project I'm working on, and the fact that Pudge is probably going to come live with me soon, and yeah, you could say that I've got few things on my mind."

Izzy immediately stopped walking. "What did you say?"

"I said a lot of things."

"I'm specifically referring to the thing you said about Pudge living with you."

"Don't tell me you think it's a bad idea, too?"

"It's not that," said Izzy. "It's the simple fact that you didn't come and talk to me about it first. I'm assuming that you already asked Pudge?"

"Well, yeah. We went to talk with my sociology professor about her situation, and I brought up the idea. Nothing is concrete yet, because Pudge wants to talk to her parents first to see if they'll let her come back home. But if they don't, then she's probably going to come and stay with me for a while."

"I don't believe this," said Izzy. "Why didn't you tell me you were even considering this as a possibility?"

"When have I had the chance?" Queenie argued. "It's not as if I was purposely hiding it from you or anything."

"This is such a huge step, Queenie. There are so many factors involved, including Pudge's parents, and her overall welfare. I don't think you really understand."

"I do understand, and that's exactly why I extended the offer in the first place. Where is she going to go if her parents don't let her back in? She can't keep living on the streets, you said so yourself. It's my place, foster care or a group home. And we both know how she feels about the last two."

Izzy watched as a crew team rowed past them on the adjacent Charles River, moving their oars aggressively as they headed upriver. "I don't understand why you couldn't talk to me about this," she said. "I thought you and I had a connection, but you went ahead and did this without even consulting me first."

"It's not as if we're dating or anything," Queenie said bitterly. "Why would I need to consult you about anything?"

Izzy stared up at Queenie with tightened lips. "Dating or not, I care deeply about Pudge. The least you could have done is to respect that."

She turned to go, but Queenie reached out and took

her tenderly by the arm before she could take a single step. "Wait—don't go. You're right. I'm sorry that I said that. I just feel like everyone I'm close to is constantly questioning me lately. It's like no one thinks I'm responsible enough, even after everything I've done and accomplished this semester. And that hurts."

Even though she was wearing mittens, Izzy put her hands in the pockets of her coat to keep them warm. "I never said that you were irresponsible."

"I know, I know," Queenie replied. She took a deep breath and slowly let it out, watching as the warm air formed a cloud in front of her as it left her mouth. "I should have talked to you first to let you know what was going on. But everything sort of happened so fast and there wasn't a good time to bring it up." She took a few steps forward. "I can't go back on it now; I already made the offer to Pudge."

"What did she say?"

"Not much. But I think it made her feel good to know that living with me was a realistic option. As soon as she's ready, we're going to go and talk with her parents."

"You're really serious about this?"

"Of course I am. I wouldn't have offered in the first place. Just like I wouldn't have volunteered at the shelter, if I weren't serious."

Izzy shielded herself from the wind. "I think that one of the social workers from the shelter should come with you when Pudge goes and talks with her parents," she said after a moment. "There should be someone there who has experience with these types of situations to mediate the conversation."

"I agree. I already promised Professor Duncan that I wouldn't go with Pudge alone, and that I'd make sure a social worker was with me."

"Just when I think I've got you all figured out, you continue to surprise me," said Izzy. "When I first met you,

I certainly never expected you to be as involved with Pudge as you are now. Honestly, even when I signed you up as a volunteer, I figured you'd lose interest after a week or so."

"I know. But I was determined to prove you wrong."

"I'm sorry," Izzy said, shaking her head. "I completely misjudged you."

"Don't feel so bad," said Queenie. "Considering where I was when we first met, I wouldn't have had much faith in me, either. But meeting Pudge affected me in a way that I can't even begin to explain. And I'm not about to turn my back on her now."

"Even if it costs you your best friend?"

"JJ already told me that Pudge has nothing to do with her wanting to leave. She said that she feels like Boston isn't the right place for her, and that she wants to spread her wings a little bit and do her own thing. I know she used to rely on me to help her make decisions and to help boost her confidence when we were in high school. But that's all changed. She's got a lot of confidence these days—she even broke up with her girlfriend on her own. Maybe I need her more than she needs me."

Queenie approached Izzy slowly, easing closer to her face. "Look, I'm sorry for venting like that. I want you to know that I was planning on telling you about Pudge. We've both been so busy, and there hasn't been a good time."

"I suppose I can forgive you." Izzy relaxed into a smile. "But that doesn't mean you can't still make it up to me."

"Okay, how about dinner in the North End next Friday night? My treat."

"Would this be a real date?"

"Depends."

"On what?"

"On your response," Queenie teased.

Izzy tossed her head back and laughed sweetly. "I'd love

to go out to dinner with you," she said as she licked her cold lips. "But you do know what this means now, don't you?"

"That I have to consult you on things from now on?"

"You got it."

CHAPTER 19

JJ stood below the basketball rim at the playground, laying the ball forcefully against the backboard and into the net. She did ten reps on the right side and ten reps on the left side, just like they used to do in practice back at Sampson Academy. Then she stepped back to the foul line, dribbled three times and shot the ball. It clanked against the front of the rim and bounced back to her.

"Use your legs more," Queenie advised. She had been watching JJ quietly from a park bench adjacent to the basketball courts for at least ten minutes. "You're not following through with the legs."

JJ dribbled the ball three times before shooting again, and this time she made sure to extend her legs as she released the ball. It sank through the net.

"That's it," said Queenie as she made her way over.

"You could be a coach," JJ replied.

"No way, I don't have the dedication. Remember Coach Cook? She ate, breathed and slept basketball."

"She's also the reason we won back-to-back championship seasons."

"Really? I thought I was the reason," said Queenie.

JJ tried to hold in her laughter, but she couldn't. It oozed out of her. "Why do you have to be so funny all of the time? It's hard to stay mad at you when you're making me laugh."

"Laughter is the best medicine. Who wants to stay mad? It's unhealthy to hold grudges."

"Who said I was holding a grudge?"

Queenie snatched the basketball out of JJ's hands. "I was referring to myself." She dribbled in for an easy lay-up. "How about a friendly game of one-on-one?"

"Don't you think we should talk first?"

"Talk is cheap."

"Seriously?"

"Okay, let's talk," said Queenie. "I was out of line the other day, I know that. I get it, all right? You don't feel at home here and wanting you to stay when you want to leave is selfish of me. I should have been more understanding when you first told me you were transferring to Smith." Her shoulders slumped forward regrettably. "I kind of got the feeling that you felt out of place here. I just didn't want to hear you actually say it because that would make it real. I'm used to having you around all the time to keep me in line, and I don't like the thought of you not being here."

"But you don't need me to keep you in line anymore, Queenie. You're doing that all by yourself. Look at everything you've accomplished so far this semester and the changes you've made. It's incredible. You said you were going to prove everyone wrong and you have."

"I know. But I also know that I've been too wrapped up with my own life to stop and consider what you've been going through."

"I'm actually glad that you've been so busy," said JJ. "It forced me to deal with some things on my own. I should be thanking you, because it gave me the confidence to know that I can take care of myself. We just don't need each other the way we did in high school. Maybe it's time we gave each other space to grow?"

"You make it sound like we've been dating or something."

"We spend so much time together that most people think we are dating."

"You're totally not my type," said Queenie. She heaved

the basketball at the net with a hook shot. It swirled around the rim and bounced out.

"Trust me," said JJ. "The feeling is quite mutual."

"Even so, I can't imagine not seeing you every day."

"It's not like I'm moving to another country or anything. I'm only going to be an hour and a half away from here. Northampton is practically right around the corner. And whenever you need a break from the city, you always can come and stay with me."

"You sure this has nothing to do with me asking Pudge to live with me?"

"I swear. I'm doing this because it's something that I want to do. I'll admit that I think letting Pudge move in with you is a crazy idea, but you know her better than I do and if you think it can work then I believe you. She can even have my room when I move out."

"Nothing is for certain yet. She might not even need to move in with me if her parents let her come home."

"Do you think they will?"

"I don't know," said Queenie. She tossed the ball into the air, caught it and twirled it on her finger before passing it across the court to JJ. "We'll see what happens."

"Well, no matter what happens," JJ dribbled the ball back and forth between her legs, "I promise to be there for you. But you have to promise to help me move all my stuff to Northampton before spring semester starts."

"Deal." Queenie stepped forward on the blacktop, positioning herself directly in front of JJ. "Now, how about that game?"

CHAPTER 20

Pudge stumbled sleepily into the dining room of the shelter. It was early Friday morning, and she had been suffering bouts of insomnia for over a week. Her eyes danced around the room, finally landing on the back of Queenie's golden-blonde head. Queenie sat at a table in the far left corner, drinking coffee from a Styrofoam cup. JJ was sitting at the table beside her.

"What are you guys doing here so early?" Pudge asked when she reached the table.

"Enjoying a not-so-fresh cup of coffee before we head off to class. I needed to stop by and talk to Izzy for a moment." Queenie adjusted the collar on her shirt. "We have our first official date tonight."

"It's about time," Pudge yawned. She sat down and turned to JJ without saying hello. "What are you reading?"

"*Oliver Twist*," JJ replied, looking up from the book.

"It's about an orphan, right?"

"Yes. It's a classic." JJ placed a napkin in between the pages of the book and closed it. "I saw it in the library the other day, and I realized that I had never actually read the whole book."

"Do you like to read a lot?"

"Sometimes I do. Depends on what kind of a mood I'm in."

"Actually, she likes to write a lot," Queenie said. "She's pretty talented."

"What do you write?"

"Poetry, mostly. But I'm trying a few other things. I'm

hoping to finish my first novel soon."

"A novel?" Pudge's eyes grew wide. "Like, a whole book?"

JJ nodded.

"Wow," said Pudge. "I haven't read a book in a long time."

"How come?"

"It's hard to read books when you have nowhere to keep them."

"Don't they have any books here at the shelter?"

"They have a few, but the selection is kind of small. Izzy said they don't have the money right now to get new books." Pudge pointed at the book in JJ's hands, "Think I could read that one after you're finished with it?"

"Here," said JJ as she handed the book over. "You can read it now if you want. I've seen the movie hundreds of times. I already know what happens."

Pudge took the book and ran her hands gingerly over the cover. "Does it have a happy ending? Does the orphan end up finding a new family?"

"I don't want to spoil it for you," said JJ. "Let's just say that things work out for the best."

"I hope things work out for the best for me, too."

"Why wouldn't they?"

Pudge didn't respond. She just kept staring at the book in her hands.

"Hey, I've got to get to class," JJ said to Queenie as she pushed her chair back from the table.

Queenie picked up her cell phone to check the time. "Yeah, me too. I'll catch up with you outside." She turned to Pudge. "We've got to get going. How about you walk me to the front door?"

Pudge rose from her seat slowly, clutching the book tightly in her hands as they walked through the dining room. "You were right about her," she said once they reached the foyer of the building. "She is cool."

"JJ? I told you. You think I would be friends with someone who wasn't cool?"

When Pudge didn't laugh, Queenie knew something was wrong.

"Hey?" she asked gently. "What's up?"

"Nothing," Pudge replied quietly. "I've just been thinking a lot about my parents." She stared up at Queenie. "I want to go see them."

"Right now?"

"Not right this second," said Pudge. "But soon. I don't think that I can wait much longer. I know I act like it's a lot of fun living on the streets, and that it doesn't bother me. But that's just me pretending so I don't think about how much I want to go back home. I miss my parents. And I was thinking the other night that maybe they miss me, too. Maybe they want me to come home as much as I want to go home."

"Maybe," said Queenie.

"I know you said I could live with you, but I really just want to go home. I see other kids on the street all the time that look so happy with their families. They're clean, they're dressed in nice clothes and they're having fun with their parents. I want that. I don't want to be homeless anymore."

"Okay," said Queenie. "Let me talk to one of the social workers here at the shelter first. Then we'll go see your parents."

Pudge began to say something then stopped. "Queenie," she managed. "I'm scared of what they are going to say. What if they don't want me back?"

"I know you're scared," said Queenie. "But no matter what happens, you've got me. I'm not going anywhere, I promise you that. And the offer to come stay with me still stands. I'll be with you every step of the way. We can figure this whole thing out together. You don't have to deal with this by yourself."

"I think meeting you was the best thing that happened to me since I left home."

"That's interesting," said Queenie. "Because I think that meeting you was the best thing that has ever happened to me in my whole life. I mean it, Pudge. I'm a better person today because of you."

Without a word, Pudge leapt up and wrapped her arms around Queenie, squeezing her tight. Queenie patted her awkwardly on the back at first, and then slowly relaxed into a hug. She didn't like to get emotional, but in that moment it was hard not to reflect on the real world education she was receiving outside of her classroom walls.

Her experience with Pudge had been an in-your-face, tough, blunt kind of education. It was bittersweet, overwhelming and head-spinning. Sometimes, it almost seemed too much to bear. But coming from where she had been, Queenie knew it was the exact kind of education she needed most.

While standing there locked in a sisterly embrace with Pudge, she knew she wouldn't change it for anything.

Queenie paced back and forth across the smooth, dark hardwood that lined the apartment floor. Every so often, she would stop in front of the window and push the curtains aside, and then turn and begin pacing some more.

"You need to relax," said JJ, who was watching her from the couch with much amusement. "Being anxious about it isn't going to help. I should know. It only makes the situation worse."

"I know," said Queenie. "I never get nervous about anything, especially when it comes to something like this.

I'm just afraid of messing it all up."

"You're not going to mess it up. But I'm glad you decided to listen to me and get a limo. When is the driver picking you up?"

"He should be here any minute now." Queenie made her way over to the window once more and looked out at the street below. "I feel like I'm going to be sick." She placed two fingers on her neck. "My pulse is going crazy. Is this normal?"

"It's called anticipation. Now you know why I could never eat before a basketball game."

"This isn't some silly basketball game."

"I was just trying to make a point."

"I'm sorry," Queenie said as she shook her head from side to side. "I don't know what's wrong with me."

"What happened to the girl who is always so carefree? Who used to laugh at me when I was a mess over Kendal, and who used to tell me to just go with the flow, 'because in the big scheme of things, nothing really matters and it's all just a means to an end?' "

"I would just like to point out that your sarcasm isn't going unnoticed," Queenie said blandly.

"Remember back at Sampson, when you poured cold water on my head right before I had to read my poem out loud in front of everyone at the coffee shop for my writing class?"

"Yes."

"Now, we're even." JJ placed her arms casually behind her head. "I don't get why you are so nervous in the first place. Girls have a history of throwing themselves in your lap. It's almost sickening."

"You know that Izzy isn't like that," Queenie said. "Look how long it took for me to ask her out on a date." She walked away from the window and sat down next to JJ. "What if I'm not ready for this?"

"Ready for what? A relationship?"

"Yes. You know I'm not the kind of person who buys flowers and writes romantic poems and does all of that sappy romantic stuff. I've never even been in a real relationship before. What do I know about treating a girl right?"

"You *are* ready. I can feel it, and it's clear that Izzy is the perfect girl for you." JJ pointed to the bouquet of roses on the coffee table. "Look, you've already taken my advice and bought her flowers. Plus, you rented a limo and you're taking her to dinner at one of the most expensive restaurants in the North End. If you ask me, you're doing just fine."

"You think so?"

"Trust me. I don't know any girl who wouldn't appreciate a fancy limousine and a beautiful bouquet of roses on a first date. Every girl likes to be wined and dined every once in awhile."

A car horn erupted from the street below. Queenie jumped up and rushed back over to the window. "There's the limo driver," she said, before taking a deep breath. "Here goes nothing."

CHAPTER 21

The last thing Izzy expected to see when she walked outside of her apartment was a smooth black stretch-limousine parked in front of the building. It sat idling next to the curb, looking ostentatious in the lower-middle-class neighborhood where she lived.

Queenie didn't seem to notice. She was standing proudly off to the side of the vehicle with the large bouquet of roses in her hands, dressed in black pants, a cobalt blue button-down shirt and a black dinner jacket. Her golden-blonde hair was tucked back in a ponytail, underneath a black newsboy cap.

Izzy shuffled awkwardly toward her, feeling completely underdressed in her dark blue jeans, a long-sleeved black blouse, and a bold red pea coat and matching red flats.

"Hey, beautiful," Queenie said as she offered Izzy the roses. "Ready for the night of your life?"

Izzy hesitated slightly before responding with a smile, and climbing into the limo. She considered the leather interior, the champagne bottle chilling next to them in the ice bin, and the bouquet of roses sitting on her lap as Queenie slid into the seat next to her.

"So—what do you think?"

"I think I'm a little underdressed for the occasion," said Izzy.

"Nonsense. You look great. We're going high class tonight."

"I see that. It's, um, all very nice."

"I wanted to impress you."

Izzy forced another smile. "You should know by now that you don't have to try and impress me," she said. "I like you just the way you are."

"Yeah, but this is different."

"How so?"

"It's our first date. I wanted to do it up just right."

"You know I don't care about that kind of stuff," said Izzy. "We could have eaten at a hot dog vendor in the middle of Boston Common, and spent the evening lying on a blanket and gazing at the stars. That would have been just as right."

"Seriously, a hot dog vendor? That's ridiculous. Every girl wants to be wined and dined every once in awhile."

"Not this girl," said Izzy with a slight edge to her voice. "I work at a homeless shelter, Queenie. When you see the things that I see day in and day out, you come to realize that material things and excess just aren't that important."

"Come on," said Queenie. "What's wrong with a little indulgence every now and again? Besides, it's all on my dime."

"Don't you mean your parents' dime?"

Queenie winced and turned abruptly in her seat. "What's wrong with you tonight? I'm just having a little fun. I thought you'd enjoy an expensive night out for a change."

"If that's what you thought then you obviously don't know me very well. I'm not just some random girl you met at the club who gets turned on by your bling and your smooth talk, remember?"

"You know I don't think that."

"Then why would you feel the need to go overboard with all of this?" Izzy held up the roses and pointed at the champagne. "This kind of stuff doesn't impress me at all. I don't even drink."

"Aren't you overreacting just a bit? Buying flowers and champagne isn't a crime. JJ does it all the time."

"Yes, but I bet JJ does it to be sweet, and not to get something in return."

Queenie's mouth dropped wide open. "You still think I

try to bribe people to get what I want?"

"You said it yourself—you used to do it all the time."

"Yeah, I *used* to do it. But I don't anymore. I told you that because I was being honest and upfront with you. If I were going to try and bribe you to be with me, why would I have told you that in the first place?"

"I'm just a little confused," said Izzy. "This is exactly the reason why I gave you such a hard time when we first met, because I thought you were materialistic and shallow."

"You know that I'm not like that at all. I only did all of this to let you know how much I care about you. I've never been on a date before with someone I really liked, and I thought this is what I needed to do."

"All you *needed* to do was be yourself," said Izzy. "Remember that day when you took me out for a cup of coffee? You were so honest and open. You checked your ego at the door. You didn't try to impress me then. That's the Queenie I fell for, and that's the Queenie I looked forward to seeing all those times at the shelter." She handed Queenie back the flowers and asked the limo driver to pull over to the nearest curb.

"I'm sorry," Izzy said as she opened the limo door. "But that's the Queenie I wanted to be with tonight. Not this one."

"What are you doing home already?" JJ asked. She was still sitting on the couch in the same relaxed position she was in when Queenie had left.

"Remember all that advice you gave me about how to impress a girl on the first date?" Queenie asked as she sulked into the room with her shirt untucked, still carrying the bouquet of roses.

"Um, yeah?"

"I think that maybe you should just keep it to yourself next time."

"Why? What happened?"

Queenie plopped down on the couch. "I totally bombed, that's what happened." She tossed the roses at JJ. "Here, you can have the flowers. I don't need them." In desperation, she buried her face in her hands. "I should have known better. Izzy doesn't care about flowers and all that other stuff. I don't know what I was thinking. Instead of impressing her, I totally repulsed her."

"Wait, you repulsed her by giving her flowers? That doesn't make any sense."

"It's not about the flowers."

"Then what is it about? I don't understand?"

"Remember when I first met Pudge, and I tried to give her money because I thought that would fix everything? Izzy's the one who called me out on it. When she first met me, I gave her the impression that I was materialistic, shallow and didn't care about anyone but myself. It wasn't until after I started spending time at the shelter and with Pudge that she changed her mind."

"Exactly. And by now she should know that you aren't like that at all."

"Yeah, but the only thing I accomplished tonight was reinforcing her initial belief. Now she probably doesn't know what to think about me. I completely blew any opportunity I had with her."

"Give it a couple of days. I'm sure it will blow over."

"I highly doubt that." Queenie removed her hat and tossed it across the room. "Who am I kidding? I'm not meant to be in a relationship. I don't have the patience for it. It's more fun being single. Women are far too complicated."

"Are you saying that because you mean it, or because are

you just trying to make yourself feel better?"

Queenie shot JJ a look. "What do you think?"

CHAPTER 22

The last thing JJ wanted to do was skip out on her writing class, especially when she had been working so hard on her novel project lately. But she figured she'd owed it to Queenie to try and talk to Izzy, especially since the whole limo and flower mess was technically her fault. If a simple apology was going to get Queenie back in Izzy's good graces then missing class was worth it.

When she arrived at the shelter, JJ immediately noticed that the entire foyer of the building was plastered from floor to ceiling with Halloween decorations. There were fake spider-webs and ghosts hanging everywhere, and pumpkins were piled in every corner.

"What are you doing here?" a familiar, scrappy voice said from above. JJ looked up and saw Pudge peering down at her from a ladder, carefully hanging orange and black streamers from a light fixture.

"I'm looking for Izzy. Is she here?"

"She's over there," said Pudge.

JJ followed the length of her finger to the far corner of the foyer, where Izzy was busy setting up a scarecrow display. "Thanks," she said.

It didn't take long for JJ to pick up on the fact that Izzy was extremely stressed out. She was pointing at boxes, giving directions and answering lots of questions simultaneously.

While casually lingering nearby, JJ swung her arms and clasped her hands together thinking of something clever to say. Izzy barely acknowledged her presence as she bent down to finish tying a knot around the scarecrow's feet.

"Getting into the spirit of Halloween?" JJ asked when the moment presented itself.

"We have a Halloween party for our teens every year," Izzy explained, without looking away from the scarecrow. "Decorations are necessary." She stood up and brushed her hands on her jeans.

"It looks nice," said JJ. "Very festive."

"Is there something I can help you with?" Izzy asked roughly. "If you're looking for Queenie, she isn't here."

"I'm not here to see Queenie. Believe it or not, I'm actually here to see you."

"I see." Izzy bit her lip. "Did her royal highness send you here to beg me to forgive her?"

"No," JJ stiffened. "I came on my own. But really, isn't royal highness a bit much? Don't you think you're being a little harsh?"

Izzy shook her head. "I'm not wasting my time with someone like that."

"Someone like what?" JJ questioned. "Someone who buys you flowers? Someone who tries to make your first date as memorable as possible? Someone who likes and respects you so much that she goes above and beyond the call of duty to prove that she's good enough for you before she even asks you out?"

"When you put it like that, it sounds—"

"Like maybe she's not the one who should have to apologize?"

"Okay, I may have been a little hard on her. I can own up to that. It takes me a while to let someone in. I really thought she and I had a connection. But after the other night, it's obvious to me that we have very different perspectives on certain things."

"And it's obvious to me that you both really like each other.

This whole thing is getting blown way out of proportion."

Izzy turned to address another staff member's question about where to hang the Happy Halloween sign. Then she returned her attention to JJ. "Look, I appreciate you coming here to talk to me on Queenie's behalf. But as you can see, we have a lot going on today, and I need to make sure this place is ready for the Halloween party tonight."

"I can see that you're busy," said JJ. "I can also see that you're making a big mistake. You think pushing Queenie away before things get too serious will keep you from getting hurt, when actually it's going to keep you from getting to know someone really special. From my perspective, it seems like you're looking for an excuse to jump ship."

"You don't know anything about me."

"I know enough to know why Queenie likes and respects you so much. She's been my best friend since our freshman year of high school. And in all the time that we've known each other, she's never been as open and honest with any girl as she has been with you. You two have something really great sitting right in front of you. Don't let something as silly as a limo and roses ruin it. You'll only end up regretting it."

"I doubt that." Izzy turned to walk away, but JJ blocked her path.

"This whole thing is my fault," she blurted out. "Queenie was a nervous wreck because she didn't want to mess anything up, so I told her to do certain things to make a good impression—like rent a limo. I know now that I should have let her do her own thing, and the outcome probably would have been much different. I'm the one who should be apologizing. Not Queenie."

"She was nervous?"

"Nervous is an understatement. She was nearly flipping out. Izzy, she really likes you. I've never seen her act this way before. She's never been in a real relationship, and she's already told you things that she's only ever told me, probably more. I don't think you realize what a big step that is for Queenie. I know you feel the same way about her, too. Please give her another chance."

Izzy's face softened. "It's hard to say no to you when you're looking at me like that." She mindlessly played with her hair and sighed. "All right. Tell Queenie to come to the shelter tonight for the Halloween party. I'm going to be busy for the rest of the day, so we can sit down and talk about everything then."

"Great," said JJ. As she was about to leave, Izzy called after her.

"There's one last thing you can't forget to tell Queenie," she said.

"What's that?" JJ asked.

"Halloween costumes are mandatory."

Queenie emerged from her room and examined herself from head to toe in the floor length mirror hanging in the hallway. "What do you think?" she asked.

"If you're trying to get back on Izzy's good side, showing up in a *Scream* costume probably isn't the best idea," said JJ. "You look a little demented."

"Remember what happened the last time I took your advice?"

"Why did you ask me my opinion then?" JJ asked, as she slumped back against the wall. "I know Izzy said that costumes were mandatory and everything, but couldn't you find something else?"

"Today is Halloween," Queenie explained from behind the mask. "This is the only costume that was left in the entire store. Well, this and a pimp costume. But I figured the pimp costume would be a really big mistake."

"Good call. I guess a creepy *Scream* dude will have to do. Just don't scare her off before you have a chance to talk with her."

"I'm a little shocked she told you to invite me in the first place," said Queenie as she removed the mask. "I really thought I messed everything up the other night, and Izzy isn't the kind of person who changes her mind easily."

JJ slumped down further against the wall. "Well, you know, I'm sure she thought about it and realized that she was overreacting."

Queenie paused for a moment. "What were you doing at the shelter, anyway?"

"I was there to see Pudge."

"For what?"

"I wanted to check and see if she was enjoying the book I gave her."

"You went all the way down to the shelter before class to ask her about a book?"

"Not exactly." JJ shook her head and pulled herself up from the wall. "Okay, don't get mad at me or anything. But the real reason I went to the shelter was to talk to Izzy."

"Aw, JJ. Why did—"

"Because I owed you one, Queenie. I messed it up for you—the whole thing was my fault. If I had minded my own business, you would have been better off. I didn't want to see you and Izzy end over something so silly. I wanted her to know that she'd regret it if she didn't give you another chance."

"Great!" Queenie shouted, throwing the mask directly at JJ. "Now it's like I'm desperate."

"It's not like that at all," JJ maintained. "I'm the one who did all the begging. All you have to do is show up wearing a silly Halloween costume. It's a small price to pay." She handed the mask back to Queenie. "Just go and see what happens, okay? What have you got to lose?"

"My pride."

"Since when do you care about pride?"

"I don't know." Queenie tugged at the mask in her hands, kneading the rubber between her fingers. She looked intently at JJ. "Do you really think she's worth it?"

"Yeah, I do."

"I knew you were going to say that." Queenie reluctantly slid the mask back over her head and started for the front door. She turned back just before opening it. "You sure you don't want to come?"

"I'm sure." JJ picked up a bowl of Kit Kat's from the kitchen counter and held it up. "Someone has to stay here and hand out the candy. You don't need me there, anyway. I'd only get in the way. Go, have a good time, and just be your regular charming self. But I would avoid picking up any flowers along the way."

CHAPTER 23

"Welcome, ohhhahhhh, to the haunted homeless shelter!" said a boy in a ghoul mask in a low and raspy voice. He stood at the shelter entrance, hands clamped around the handle of a plastic pitchfork.

"Sam?" Queenie asked, clearly unafraid. She leaned over and tried to peek through the eyeholes of the mask. "Is that you?"

"Come on!" Sam grumbled in frustration. "Why does everyone keep guessing who I am?"

"Maybe you could try to disguise your voice a little bit."

"I am!"

"Oh," said Queenie. "Uh, I take it that the party is inside?"

"Yeah," said Sam, jabbing the pitchfork toward the entryway. He dropped his not-so-scary voice to give directions as if he were reading an ingredient label on the back of a soup can. "Follow the black arrows on the floor as you enter the haunted shelter. But beware. There are terrors along the way. If you should survive, you will be rewarded with a bag full of treats, goodies and surprises."

"Can't wait," said Queenie. She pulled her *Scream* mask over her head and walked through the door.

The black arrows on the floor were easy to identify, and they led into an adjacent room that was shadowy and dark. Queenie bent her head forward to try and get a better look at what horrors might lay ahead. She saw a path of glow sticks lined up along the floor, lighting the way through the room.

Queenie inched her way forward with her hands spread out in front of her, fully prepared to strike back if someone or something jumped out at her. She'd barely stepped into the room when a tall woman wearing a vampire costume leapt out from behind a black curtain and headed straight for her.

Queenie quickly ducked out of the way, nearly tripping over her own feet. Then something resembling a mummy moved toward her from behind. She stumbled backwards and accidentally stepped on its toe.

"Ow!"

"Sorry," said Queenie. She spun around to see if the mummy was okay and fell against a man in bloody torn clothes wielding a knife. He dropped his knife on the ground, and Queenie accidentally kicked it across the room with her foot before tripping over her cloak and falling to the floor herself.

An aged and haggard witch greeted Queenie as she rounded the corner on her hands and knees. The witch gestured toward a maze of tables and chairs that formed a path through the dining area of the shelter.

"Is there another way out of this craziness?" Queenie asked, lifting herself off the ground.

The witch responded with a few grunts and snorts, urging her to keep moving. Queenie had no choice but to brave the maze. She moved along, trying to avoid stepping on the hands that poked out from beneath the tables to grab at her black cloak.

When Queenie finally reached the entrance to the next room, she was relieved to find it fully lit and crowded with people. Orange and black streamers hung every which way from the dangling chandelier, and Halloween music blared from a stereo in the corner.

"Congratulations!" exclaimed a woman dressed in an over-the-top fairy costume. "You made it through the haunted shelter!" Queenie recognized her just as she was about to fling a bag full of candy in her direction. Her name was Linda, and she was a middle-aged volunteer who helped out at the shelter on the weekends.

"It's me, Linda." Queenie removed the mask from her face. "You don't have to give me any candy."

"Queenie?" Linda shouted above the music. "I'm so glad you could make it. Here I thought you were one of the kids."

"Have you seen Izzy?"

"She was just here." Linda turned and glanced at the crowd. "She's wearing a short black dress and heels."

"There you are!" Queenie heard a mere second before Pudge came crashing into her, grabbing her arm with both hands. "I was hoping you'd come by tonight. I have to talk to you."

"Sure," said Queenie. "But I need to talk to Izzy first. It's important."

"So is this," Pudge pleaded, tugging on Queenie's arm.

"Hey Miss Thing, where's your costume?" Linda asked. She pretended to poke Pudge in the stomach. "Costumes are mandatory, remember?"

"This is my costume," Pudge replied with a clever grin. "Can't you tell? I'm a homeless girl."

"Cute," said Queenie. "Very original."

"You can't just wear your regular clothes," said Linda. "You need to wear a costume."

"I don't care about a stupid costume," said Pudge. "I just need to talk to Queenie."

"I can't let you participate in the activities and games without a costume," Linda scolded. "There's a big box of clothes and fun masks down in the basement. Let's go find you something." She took hold of Pudge's hand.

"I said I needed to talk to Queenie first," Pudge growled, pulling her hand away.

"I'll make sure she puts on a costume," Queenie intervened. "Don't worry about it." She gently pushed Pudge off to the side. "Listen, you need to relax a little bit. I know you need to talk to me, but it's important that I talk to Izzy first. I promise to come find you as soon as soon as I'm finished." She took off her black cloak and handed it over, along with the mask. "Here, you can wear this for your costume. I'll be back in a few minutes."

"But—"

"I'll be right back," Queenie shouted over her shoulder as she disappeared into the crowd. She eventually got back to the front hallway, and then made her way down the narrow corridor that led to Izzy's office. When she reached the office, the light was on but the door was closed and the handle was locked. She knocked once and held her hands up to the glass to get a better look.

"Looking for me?"

Queenie drew back from the window to see Izzy slinking down the corridor in a short black dress, black heels and long black gloves. Her hair was smooth and slicked back with gel, and she swung her narrow hips delicately from side to side as she walked.

"Are you accosting me with your eyes?"

"What? No. Of course not," Queenie stuttered. "I . . . see, you weren't here . . . so I . . . what are you supposed to be exactly?"

Izzy withdrew a tiny plastic squirt gun from a holster on her leg and held it up. "La Femme Nikita."

"I should have known."

"Where's your costume?" Izzy asked as she regarded Queenie's street clothes. "I thought I told JJ that costumes were mandatory."

"I had on a black cloak and a *Scream* mask, but I took it off and gave it to Pudge so she could wear it instead. She didn't have a costume."

"A likely excuse," Izzy said, dangling the squirt gun from her finger.

"It's true. I nearly put myself in the hospital trying to make my way through your little house of horrors back there. I kept tripping over my own feet because I couldn't see through the mask. Ask the mummy if you don't believe me. I stepped on its toe."

Izzy burst out laughing. "I would have paid to see that. I'm really glad that you showed up." She motioned at the door with a slight nod. "Do you want to come in my office and talk? Things have calmed down a bit, and I have a few minutes."

"I thought JJ did all of the talking for me earlier today?"

"She certainly had a lot to say. The way she stuck up for you and everything was really cute." Izzy unlocked her office door and walked in. She tossed her keys on top of the desk and sat on the edge. "Anyway, she was right about one thing. I do owe you an apology."

"You do?" Queenie asked, remaining in the doorway. "You don't strike me as the kind of girl who apologizes about anything."

"The night just wasn't what I expected at all. When you picked me up in the limo, it threw me off. Everything just felt wrong. I got scared and thought that I had made a mistake about you. That's why I acted the way I did. But I think that I may have overreacted."

"Yeah, about all of that," Queenie said as she leaned her shoulder against the doorframe. "I don't know what I was thinking. I've never acted so out of character in my entire life. The truth is that I've never really been on a real date before. I'm not used to this relationship stuff. So I wanted everything to be perfect. I did stuff I thought most girls would like, instead of focusing on what *you* would like."

"It doesn't matter. I know that your heart was in the right place, and I'm sorry for being such a jerk to you about it."

Queenie shook away the apology with a flick of her wrist. "I deserved it. I should have known better."

"No one deserves to be treated like that," said Izzy. Then she tilted her head back and added, "Not even you."

Queenie laughed softly, and took a few more steps into the office. She took her time, scanning the posters and pictures hanging on the wall, before she looped back around.

"So, now what?" she asked, stopping directly in front of Izzy.

"Do you think we should try again?"

"I wouldn't mind."

Izzy sighed. "Every time we've tried to hang out somewhere besides the shelter, it's been a disaster."

"True," Queenie said, as she leaned in closer, placing her hands on the desk on either side of Izzy. "Maybe we should just walk away now and save ourselves the aggravation."

"I couldn't agree more," Izzy played along.

"There's just one small problem."

"What's that?"

"I'd really like to kiss you right now," said Queenie.

Izzy held Queenie's stare as she slowly reached up and clasped her hands around the back of Queenie's neck. "Then what are you waiting for?" Izzy asked, with a sly smile.

Queenie spent the next hour at the shelter hunting for Pudge, but couldn't find her anywhere. She wasn't bobbing for apples, she wasn't dancing on the makeshift dance floor and she wasn't mingling with the group of bored teens in the back hallway, either. As much as she hated to do it, Queenie even inched through the haunted house section of the shelter again while calling out Pudge's name, nearly knocking over a display of fake gravestones in the process.

By the time she arrived back in the foyer, she had given up. As she stepped outside of the building, she noticed that Sam was still positioned at his greeting post. He was sitting on the front steps instead of standing at the door, and he'd taken off the ghoul mask.

"You're still out here?" she asked. "Why haven't you come in to join the party?"

"I hate crowds," he replied. "It's nice out here. You can even see the stars." He edged his body over slightly to the right. "You can sit down here with me if you want."

"Actually, I'm looking for Pudge. Have you seen her? She'd probably be wearing a *Scream* costume."

"Yeah, I just saw her outside a little while ago when she left the party."

"She left the party? Why? Where was she going?"

"I don't know. She didn't tell me." Sam scratched at his tangled, curly red hair. "She just kept mumbling something about how she had a plan. And that tonight was the perfect night for it, because it's Halloween."

"I don't believe it," Queenie said, raising both hands to her head. "She went to see her parents."

"I thought it was kind of funny that she was still wearing her costume when she left. That *Scream* mask is creepy."

"Sam, it's really important that I find her." Queenie crouched down on her knees in front of him. "Do you know where her parents live? Try to remember."

"I think they live in a ground floor apartment in Dorchester," Sam replied. "On Foster Street or something like that."

"Foster Street? Are you sure?"

Sam cocked his head, "Or maybe it was Forest Street."

"Which one is it?"

"I can't remember," he said with an apologetic shrug.

Queenie exhaled in frustration. "Why didn't I let her talk to me when I had the chance?" she uttered under her breath.

"Huh?"

"Never mind. I'm going to look for her. But do me a favor. Don't tell Izzy about this, okay? I don't want her to worry about Pudge."

Sam lifted himself up off the step. "What do I tell her if she asks where you guys are?"

"Tell her that I took Pudge trick-or-treating or something."

"You want me to lie?" he asked.

"You aren't lying."

"Then what am I doing?"

Queenie skipped down the steps two at a time. "Buying me some time," she returned without looking back.

CHAPTER 24

Sam had been right the first time. The street name was Foster, and it didn't take long for Queenie to catch sight of Pudge in her *Scream* costume hiding behind a parked car next to the curb. She must have been sitting there for at least an hour.

When Queenie first stepped out of the cab, she didn't think she'd be able to find Pudge in the dark, let alone mixed in with all of the other kids trick-or-treating up and down the street. She wasn't even sure if Pudge would still be there. But the hunched over figure planted behind a green Ford Escape that was parked awkwardly in its space was definitely Pudge. The girl was staring intensely at the front porch of a two-story red building across the street.

The light inside the ground level apartment was on and every time the doorbell rang, a heavyset middle-aged woman with drab brown hair greeted the trick-or-treaters on her porch with a welcoming smile.

Queenie took a few calculated steps and crept up quietly behind the SUV. "You could have let me know that this was the plan you had in mind," she whispered harshly.

Pudge spun around so fast that she almost fell over. "What are you trying to do?" she hissed. "Give me a heart attack?"

"I could ask you the same thing," said Queenie as she bent down beside the SUV. "I thought we agreed you weren't going to run away again?"

"I wasn't running away. I came to see my parents."

"You could have let me know."

"You didn't have time to listen, remember?" Pudge batted her eyes mockingly, "You wanted to talk to your girlfriend, Izzy."

"Cut that out," Queenie warned. "It was important."

"So is this."

"What is 'this' exactly? *Mission Impossible*? You can't hide behind a car all night. Someone is going to see you and call the cops because it looks downright creepy. They'll mistake you for a burglar or something."

"Let them think what they want."

Queenie lowered her head to one side. "I'm serious, Pudge. You can't sit out here like this all night."

"I'm waiting for the right moment." Pudge pointed at a steady stream of kids dressed in a variety of Halloween costumes, flowing from house to house. "I don't want to go ring the doorbell with a bunch of other kids around."

"Just out of curiosity, why did you tell Sam that tonight was the perfect night?"

"Because it's Halloween. They have to answer the doorbell. They won't suspect that it's me. And once they open the door and let me inside, I'll remove the mask. Then they'll have to talk to me, no matter what."

"I don't know if this is such a good idea," Queenie said, resting her arm on her knee. "Putting them on the spot like this isn't fair."

Pudge's eyes filled with resentment. "And what is fair? Kicking me out at fourteen?"

"Okay, okay. You've got a point. But don't you want to meet with them at a neutral place? We could meet them for coffee or something."

"Yeah, right. They haven't tried to look for me in almost five months. Why would they make time to come meet me for coffee?"

"I don't know." Queenie raised her head and looked around. "This whole thing feels all wrong. I'm not sure we should approach it like this."

"It doesn't matter to me what you think," said Pudge. "You can stay right here behind the car for all I care."

"Pudge, we had an agreement. When Professor Duncan finds out that you went to see your parents without a social worker present, he's going to kill me. So will Izzy."

Pudge watched as the last group of kids on the block walked up the porch steps and rang the doorbell. The chorus of "trick-or-treat" echoed into the night.

"I don't care what they think, either," she said, continuing to watch the activity on the porch. "I can't wait any longer. I want to go home and I need to know if my parents want me back or not." She jerked her head around and glared at Queenie, fighting back tears. "Can't you understand that?"

Queenie relaxed her stare, and slumped sympathetically against the bumper of the car. "Yeah," she said. "I can understand that."

Pudge planted her eyes back on the front door of the house.

"Is there anything I can do?" Queenie asked after a moment.

"Wait out front for me," said Pudge, rising slowly from her knees. "I've decided that talking to my parents is something I have to do alone." With that, she slid the mask over her face and crossed the street.

Queenie reached in her pocket for a rubber band and pulled her hair back into a ponytail. She felt her cell phone poke her in the leg and wondered if she should fish it out of her jeans and call Izzy for reinforcements.

But as soon as she saw Pudge reach forward and ring the doorbell, she knew it was too late. The door opened. Queenie craned her neck to listen in, but she was too far away to hear anything clearly. The middle-aged woman unsuspectingly welcomed Pudge into the house just as she had done for all of the other trick-or-treaters on the block.

And when the door closed behind them, all Queenie could do was hold her breath.

* * *

When the door opened, Pudge came running down the porch steps at full speed, without her costume. Queenie instantly leapt to her feet and caught up with her on the sidewalk a block away.

"What happened?" she asked.

"What do you think happened? They don't want me to come home unless I give up this 'lifestyle.' "

"Lifestyle? As if you had a choice?"

"Yeah, that's what my dad calls it. Can you believe that?"

Queenie reached out to give her a hug, but Pudge pushed her away. "Don't," she said. "I want to be alone right now."

"That's the last thing you need."

"Stop trying to tell me what I need!"

"Okay, I'm sorry. What did they say? Tell me what happened."

Pudge kicked at a pebble on the sidewalk and let out an animated growl.

"That bad?"

"Worse," Pudge returned. She collapsed onto the grass, picked a maple leaf up and began to shred it. Queenie didn't move.

Pudge scooped up a second leaf, picked at it, sighed and finally asked, "Do you want to know what happened or not?"

"Of course," Queenie replied, quickly dropping down on the sidewalk next to her.

"When my mom invited me inside, she had no idea it was me," Pudge began quietly. "She thought I was one of the neighborhood kids. Then she grabbed the bowl of candy, and realized that I didn't have a bag with me. I think she started to get nervous, so I told her that I had a Halloween surprise for her."

"I'm sure that calmed her right down," Queenie slipped in.

"I could tell she was really uncomfortable at that point so I took off my mask and I said, 'Surprise, Mom, it's me!' She was surprised all right."

"What did she do?"

"She dropped the bowl of candy on the floor and gave me a hug. I thought everything was going to be okay, but then my dad came into the room and it didn't go so well after that."

Pudge scoured the ground for another leaf. She didn't have to look too hard, since both the grass and sidewalk were littered with a colorful array of leaves.

"My father walks in, takes one look at me and asks me where I've been. I told him I had been living on the streets since the beginning of summer. Then he told me that the experience was probably good for me. I asked him what he meant and he said that it probably gave me a good glimpse of what life is like for 'those' kinds of people."

Queenie cringed.

"I told him that the experience made me realize how much I missed them and that I wanted to come home. My mom started crying and hugging me. Then my father said, 'I knew a little tough love would straighten you out.' I couldn't believe he said that."

"Interesting choice of words," said Queenie.

"So I told him that I was still gay, and that it would never change. But I also told him that I missed both of them and that I wanted to come home. I asked them if they missed me and my mom said, 'Of course we do, Sweetie.'" Pudge raised her head and looked directly at Queenie. "Then I asked them why they would kick me out of the house and not look for me all summer."

"What did she say?"

"Mom didn't say anything. She just looked at my dad, and he said that it was for my own good. He also said that if I was going to continue to choose to be gay then I wasn't welcome in their home anymore. He said I could only come home if I was ready to be the person God intended me to be. That's when I threw my mask at him and ran out the door."

"Pudge, I'm so sorry."

"It's okay."

"No, it isn't. It really isn't." Queenie placed her hands on the ground and stood up.

"You know what the funny part is?" Pudge asked. "I'm doing exactly what my father wants me to do, being the person God intended me to be. Yet, he doesn't even realize it."

"I know." Queenie reached down and helped Pudge off the sidewalk.

"What am I supposed to do now?" Pudge asked. "Where am I supposed to go?"

"You're coming home with me"

"Are you sure that's what you really want," Pudge asked as she wiped her hands on the back of her jeans.

"Of course, I'm sure. You can sleep in my room and I'll take the couch. Then we'll figure out the logistics for something long term." She nodded at the nearest bus stop. "Take the bus to my place and I'll meet you back there. JJ is home for the night so she'll let you in. Just tell her I said you could stay with us."

"Why aren't you coming with me?"

Queenie's eyes drifted back in the direction of Pudge's

parents' house. "There's something I need to do, first," she said. "And I won't be able to live with myself if I don't."

Though the front porch light had already been turned off, Queenie knocked lightly on the front door. When no one answered, she knocked again.

The porch light flicked on, and she noticed a shadowy figure stealing a quick look out the window. A few seconds later, the front door opened.

A short and slightly balding man stuck his head out from behind the screen door. "Who are you?" he asked brusquely, examining Queenie through a pair of oversized bronze glasses. She knew instantly that it was Pudge's father.

"I'm a friend of your daughter's," she answered as politely as possible.

"What do you want?"

Queenie opened her mouth to speak but she wasn't even sure what she wanted to say. She slid her hands into the front pockets of her jeans and choked back the bitterness in her throat.

"Like I said, I'm a friend of your daughter's," she managed. "I see her almost *every day* at the homeless shelter downtown. She's homesick and lost and she's—" Queenie broke off as her throat closed again.

Pudge's father gave her an impatient look.

"What I'm trying to say," she continued, "is that Pudge is an amazing, smart, kind, tough and wonderful kid. She doesn't belong on the streets. She belongs at home with her family. Can't you see that kicking her out is setting her up for disaster? You're tossing her aside like something you can throw away or give back if you don't want it. She's your daughter, sir. But, above all else, she's a human being."

Pudge's father drew in a short breath, and Queenie watched as his face transformed from a look of impatience to one of utter disgust.

"Who are you to stand here and lecture me?" he demanded, staring her down while shaking his head. Then he added with a condescending smile, "Oh, I see. You're just like she is, aren't you? I feel sorry for you. Your parents must be heartbroken."

Queenie bit her tongue. She wanted to yell and scream, grab hold of him and shake him into awareness.

"With all due respect," she said as calmly as she could, "there's no need to feel sorry for me. My parents love me and respect me for who I am, even if I do drive them a little crazy now and then. They'd still never turn their backs on me. Seeing what Pudge has had to go through since you kicked her out made me realize just how truly blessed I am to have parents who are open-minded enough to accept me for who I am. If anything, I feel sorry for you. One day you're going to look back on this and wish you could have done things much differently. I only hope that when you go looking for forgiveness, Pudge won't be as close-minded and as unforgiving as you are."

"George, who's out there?" a voice called from inside.

"It's just one of the last trick-or-treaters for the night," Pudge's father answered. Then he narrowed his eyes at Queenie and growled, "Get off my front porch before I call the police."

"There's no need to call the police," Queenie said, as she backed down the porch steps. "That's all I wanted to say. It's just something to think about, something to consider. Maybe one day, you'll get it."

Queenie could still feel his beady eyes watching her as she walked down the sidewalk. She turned around when she reached the end of the street. The porch light was still on and Pudge's father was still standing at the front door. She hoped that he was thinking about what she had said, but she had a sinking feeling he was just making sure she was gone before he finally closed the door and locked it tight.

CHAPTER 25

When JJ woke up in the morning, she untangled herself from the bed covers and stumbled into the bathroom. She splashed warm water on her face and brushed her teeth. Then she headed into the kitchen and fumbled around in the refrigerator.

With a glass of orange juice in one hand and a banana in the other, she walked into the living room to find Queenie asleep on the couch in an almost upright position. She was still wearing the same jeans and long-sleeved black waffle shirt she had been wearing under her Halloween costume the previous night.

JJ took a bite from her banana and watched Queenie for a minute as she snored slightly before each breath. Her elbow was resting against the arm of the couch and her head was squished into her hand.

"Rough night?"

Queenie awoke with a start. Her eyes darted up and around then settled on JJ. "What time is it?"

"Almost ten. You must have been out late, because I didn't even hear you come in."

"It was after one in the morning when I finally came home," Queenie said, yawning lengthily. "The last thing I remember is sitting down right here."

"Things went well with Izzy, I take it?"

"Yes, but that wasn't the reason I came home so late. I had to blow off some steam."

"Why?" JJ asked in between bites of her banana. "What

happened?" She sat down on the couch.

"Didn't Pudge tell you?"

"Why would Pudge have told me anything?"

"I assumed she would have told you when she got here last night."

"She was supposed to come here last night?"

With a befuddled look, Queenie hurried up from the couch and ran into her bedroom. After a moment, JJ heard her curse in muffled frustration. "I don't believe this," she said as she came back into the living room. "I told her to come straight here last night after everything happened."

"I'm not following you," JJ said, still confused. "What are you talking about?"

"Pudge went to see her parents last night."

"She did? Did you go with her?"

"Sort of. She went by herself without me knowing. When I found out about it, I chased her and caught up with her right outside their house. But she didn't want me to come inside with her. She said she needed to talk to them alone."

"Wow. That takes a lot of guts. What did they say?"

"They basically told her that she can't come home unless she stops being gay."

"That's like asking her to stop having green eyes," said JJ, tossing the banana peel aside.

"I know that and you know that, but her parents don't see it that way. They are still under the impression that being gay is a choice."

"I've never understood that argument," said JJ. "Why would we choose something that causes us to be ridiculed, bullied and ostracized by other people? If we had a choice, wouldn't we choose to be like everybody else, so we didn't have to go through any of that?"

Queenie sat down and leaned her head back on the couch pillow behind her. "It doesn't surprise me that she ran away again. I can't imagine what that whole experience must have been like for her. To stand there in front of her parents, pleading with them to accept and love her just as she is, only to have them kick her right back out the door. It made me sick to my stomach, and I was the one who was standing outside by the curb."

JJ remembered when she had come out to her own parents right before her junior year of high school. They'd been forced to challenge their previous set of beliefs. It took time for them to process everything, and to reach a level of understanding and acceptance. But it also gave them the opportunity to open their minds, and they finally embraced JJ's orientation fully. Not once did they threaten to kick her out or judge her for it. If anything, their love for her had only grown stronger.

"When Pudge came running out of the house afterwards, she was really upset and she told me what they said," Queenie continued. "She seemed to be okay after we talked about it for a little bit. That's when I told her to come here, so we could figure everything out."

"Maybe she went back to the shelter instead," said JJ. "Give Izzy a call."

"I'm going to. I have to fill her in on what happened. She was still at the Halloween party when all of this went down. I doubt Pudge is there, though. I have a feeling that this time she's planning on running away for good. But I have no idea where she could have gone."

"Are you okay?" asked JJ, sensing the concern in Queenie's voice.

Queenie leaned forward and bent her head down as if she were about to be sick. "Yeah, I'm okay." She turned to JJ. "It's surreal to watch something like this happen. I mean, I read articles about it in the library and stuff. But to actually see it happen to someone you care about right before your own eyes, it's agonizing to watch."

"I can imagine."

"No, you can't," Queenie snapped. "It's not something you'd want to imagine, either."

"Hey, I didn't mean—"

"I know," said Queenie, lowering her voice. "I'm a little upset right now. I really thought Pudge would stay with me. I thought she trusted me enough. But it hurts knowing that she decided to run away again instead. It's like a slap in my face."

"I'm sure she has her reasons."

"Maybe." Queenie placed on her hands on her knees and got up from the couch. "I better go call Izzy. Then I have to go look for Pudge."

JJ drank the rest of her orange juice. "Do you want me to come with you?"

"No," said Queenie. "If I manage to find her, she and I need to have a serious talk about this running away habit. It's starting to get on my nerves."

Queenie played with her cell phone as she waited for an inbound train to South Station. An hour earlier, she'd called Izzy to explain what had happened. Izzy said that Sam had seen Pudge at the shelter late last night. Pudge had asked him for some money, but Sam told her that he didn't have any. When Sam asked her what she needed it for, she said she was going to South Station to try and catch a bus.

Queenie was on her way to South Station with the hope that Pudge hadn't already been able to scrape together enough money for a bus ticket out of town. It was one of the busiest stops on the Massachusetts Bay Transportation

Authority system, so spotting Pudge could be like spotting a nickel in a blizzard.

The inbound train was packed when it finally slowed to a stop in front of her, and Queenie had to squeeze through to an open space near the back. She held on to one of the handles on the seat next to her, trying to curb her thoughts about Pudge. If she had been able to get enough money for a bus ticket, then she was long gone by now. And there would be no way to find her.

"Why didn't you just go to my place like I told you to?" Queenie grumbled to herself. She hadn't realized that she had actually said it out loud until an elderly woman standing across from her looked at her strangely and clutched her purse tightly to her chest. Queenie smiled apologetically and turned to face the window. When she finally reached South Station, she jumped off the train and sprinted to the bus area. She dashed up to the one of the clerks and asked her if they had seen a scrappy-looking teenager with reddish-brown hair and green eyes wandering around the station. The woman behind the glass shook her head "no."

Queenie thumped her hand against the counter in disappointment and spun around. She focused her eyes on the row of pay phones off to the right side, and then along the backs of the seats to the left. There, on the far seat in the corner of the room, she spied a motionless orange lump. Queenie recognized the familiar burnt-orange jacket right away and took off straight for it. But when she got there, a strange man with dreadlocks was wearing it, not Pudge.

"Where did you get this?" Queenie demanded, tugging on the sleeve of the jacket.

"It's mine," the man sneered. "Get your own jacket." He pulled his sleeve away.

"Did you get this jacket from a teenage girl?" Queenie pressed. "Did you?"

"So what if I did? What are you going to do about it, call the cops? I paid for it fair and square."

"With what?"

"My bus ticket to Hartford."

"Connecticut?"

The man revealed a toothless grin. "No, California," he answered, his voice heavy with sarcasm.

Queenie didn't waste any time responding. She ran to the display of television screens that showed the schedule of all incoming and outgoing buses, and quickly found the number of the bus headed for Hartford, Connecticut. It was set to leave in fifteen minutes.

"Gate five!" she muttered, taking off toward it. As soon as she rounded the corner, she pulled to a sudden halt. Pudge was sitting on the floor with her back against the wall and her knees pulled up to her chest. Her head rested against her shoulder and she was fast asleep. Queenie slowly stepped closer before leaning down to examine the girl to make sure she was okay. Then she fell back against the wall with a sigh of relief, and slid down to the floor.

The movement caused Pudge to stir slightly and slowly open her eyes. She reeled back and jumped up as soon as she recognized Queenie's face.

"I bet you're surprised to see me," Queenie said smartly.

"What are you doing here? How did you find me?"

"Sam told Izzy where you went because he was worried about you. Izzy was just as concerned. But me, I'm not so sure anymore. The truth is, I'm getting a little tired of chasing you around."

Pudge lowered her head. "I didn't mean to upset you. I just freaked out after seeing my parents. I didn't know where to go."

"I told you exactly where to go," said Queenie. "I said, 'Go to my place and we'll figure it all out.' What part of that didn't you get?"

"I got it, okay? And I was going to go there, but when I got on the bus I started thinking about how I have no place to live, and how I'd be getting in the way at your place, so I rode the bus to the shelter instead. But it was late when I got there, so all the beds were taken. I thought maybe I should leave Boston and try someplace else."

"Like Hartford, Connecticut? What in the world could you possibly do in Hartford?"

"I don't know." Pudge covered held herself and shivered. "I just thought it was better than sticking around here."

"I can't believe you traded your jacket for a bus ticket," Queenie said as she removed her winter coat and placed it over Pudge's shoulders. "Put this on, will you? You're freezing."

"I didn't have any money for a ticket," Pudge complained. "It was better than trying to steal it."

"That I agree with," said Queenie. "Did you spend the whole night here?"

"Yeah," said Pudge. "I slept right in this spot."

Queenie reached back and fixed her ponytail, taking in the sights and smells of the bus station. The faint scent of urine reached her nose, and she winced. "You've got to stop running away," she said. "It's not getting you anywhere. You know what happens when you keep running from something?"

"What?"

"Nothing. Nothing happens. You end up in exactly the same spot you've always been, just with different scenery."

"How would you know?"

"Because I used to run away, too."

"You?" Pudge asked in disbelief. "You used to run away? From what?"

"I never actually ran away physically," said Queenie. "I used to run away in the metaphorical sense."

"Huh?"

"I never told you this before, but I got kicked out of quite a few private schools in my day. I was actually pretty smart when it came to the school part, but I acted like I didn't care. It was my way of rebelling against my parents because I didn't agree with their high society standard of living. They would stick me in some ritzy private school that I didn't want to go to, and I'd do whatever it took to get expelled, just to rub it in their faces. But I didn't realize that I wasn't really hurting them—I was actually hurting myself. I kept running away from these amazing opportunities and I actually thought I was cool for doing it."

"When did you stop running?"

"When I met JJ at Sampson Academy," said Queenie. "She was my roommate during my freshman year, and we hit it off. I gave the school a chance and I ended up liking it a lot. School came easy to me after that and I got good grades and played sports. I had a lot of fun. But sometimes I wonder what would have happened if I had gotten kicked out again, if I hadn't stopped running." She turned and looked Pudge directly in the eyes. "You have an amazing opportunity sitting right in front of you, and I'm the one offering it. Why would you want to run away from it?"

"I don't know," said Pudge. "Part of me is scared that you'll get sick of me or something, or that you'll regret that you said I could live with you."

"I won't, I promise you."

"You don't know that for sure."

"Maybe not," said Queenie. "But if you board that bus to Hartford, then you'll never know if it would have worked out, either. I had no idea if Sampson Academy was going to work out, but if I hadn't given it a chance and got myself kicked out, I know I'd be someplace a lot different than Boston University. I might have dropped out of high school altogether."

"Yeah, right," said Pudge.

"Seriously. I know that you're scared. I was even this close," Queenie raised two fingers together, "to flunking out of college because I was scared. I was afraid I'd never figure out what I wanted to do with my life. But I realized that I had an amazing opportunity to get a really good education, and that the rest would figure itself out."

A voice broke over the loudspeaker, announcing that the bus to Hartford was ready for boarding. Pudge stared out the window at the Greyhound carrier.

"I can't tell you what to do," said Queenie. "But I can tell you that if you come and stay with me, you'll have a welcoming place to call home and someone who cares a lot about you as your roommate. That sounds a lot better than going to some random city where you don't know anyone, and the best you can hope for is a life on the streets." She bumped her shoulder lightly into Pudge. "Come on, what do you say?"

"All right," Pudge said, as the announcer made the last call for boarding. "I'll give it a shot."

"I think you're making the right decision," said Queenie, lifting herself off the floor. "Now, let's see if we can get your jacket back.

Pudge looked at Queenie and made a face. "Let him keep the jacket. I'll even give him his ticket back."

"Why are you being so generous all of a sudden?"

"Because he probably needs the jacket more than I do." Then Pudge smirked and added, "And I know you'll want to buy me a new jacket anyway."

CHAPTER 26

"How's the project coming along," Professor Duncan asked.

"That's what I came to talk to you about," said Queenie. They were sitting in his office after class. "The project itself is going really well. I'll be ready to present by the due date for sure. But, as far as Pudge is concerned, there's been a new development."

"Oh?" Professor Duncan asked inquisitively. "And what might this new development be?"

"Pudge sort of, you see, she kind of—"

"Queenie, what's going on? I don't think I've ever seen you stumble your way through a sentence before."

"Okay. Pudge went to see her parents on Halloween. But she did it without telling me first. I know I was supposed to make sure a social worker was there with her, but she wanted to do it by herself and I couldn't stop her."

"And?"

"It was a complete disaster. They told her that they don't want her to come home unless she stopped being gay. And that isn't going to happen. So that pretty much leaves foster care or my place. And we know how she feels about foster care."

Professor Duncan folded his hands neatly in front of him. "Are you sure you're up to this? It's one thing to be her friend, but it's another thing completely to let her live and function under your roof. Pudge is going to need some kind of parental supervision and guidance."

"I can handle it," Queenie asserted. "And I also know how big of a responsibility it is. I plan on bringing her with me when I go home for Thanksgiving. Then I'll explain everything to my parents so that they are aware of the situation. I'll make sure Pudge goes to school and that she does her homework and all of that. Right now, staying with me is the best option for her."

"And you'll be able to keep up with your own school work at the same time?"

"It will be my number one priority."

Professor Duncan kept his eyes planted on Queenie's, almost as if they were stuck in an intense staring contest.

"I've already proven you wrong once," she warned him. "I don't think it would be wise to bet against me again."

When Professor Duncan started laughing, she knew she had him convinced. "Okay, you've got me there," he said. "If you think you can handle this then there is nothing more I can say. I know how invested you are. Do you plan on applying for legal guardianship?"

"I'm not sure. We'll see what happens. I can always apply for temporary guardianship in case her parents change their minds and let her come home again. As long as she has a place to stay, I'm happy."

"Pudge is very lucky to have you in her life."

"I'm lucky to have her in mine," said Queenie. "If I hadn't met her, I would have probably flunked out of college by now."

"I highly doubt that. But I'm glad to see that she has had such an impact on you. I'm looking forward to seeing your presentation."

"And I'm looking forward to getting an A in your class."

"What makes you think you're getting an A?"

Queenie looked at him as if to say, "*Really?*"

"What?" Professor Duncan asked.

"You owe me an A."

"I owe you an A? For what?"

"For all the hard work I've put in."

Professor Duncan rose from his desk chair and opened the office door. "If you get an A in my class it's because you've earned it," he said as they left the room. "Not because I *owe* it to you."

"Well in that case, I think I've earned it," said Queenie.

"Maybe you should be taking introductory law courses after all," Professor Duncan chuckled. "You already know how to argue like a lawyer."

CHAPTER 27

"Can I ask you something?" Pudge glanced at Queenie as they drove along the rolling suburban streets of Richmond, Virginia, in Queenie's black BMW. "Why do you take public transportation in Boston when you have a cool car like this?"

"I hate driving in Boston," said Queenie. "It's too confusing. There are one-way streets everywhere, and taxis always ride your bumper. People even beep at you to move when the light is still red. It's incredibly stressful. Who wants to deal with all of that?"

"Yeah, but who cares! This is really nice car."

"Then you can drive it instead."

"I can?"

"Sure, why not? I basically keep it parked in the garage at my apartment for longer trips like this anyway," Queenie explained. "I don't mind taking the subway or hopping in a cab. I figure if I'm going to live in a big city then I might as well do it right. And that includes using public transportation. So, when you get your driver's license, you can take it out for a spin."

"You'd really let me drive it whenever I—" Pudge's jaw dropped onto the floor mat of the car the moment they pulled into the long and winding driveway that led up to Queenie's family estate. Astonished, she forgot all about the BMW.

"This is your house?" she asked, wide-eyed, practically drooling.

"Yep," said Queenie, circling around a meticulously

landscaped cul-de-sac and parking in front of the five-car garage. "Home sweet home."

"It's a mansion!" Pudge exclaimed, taking in the grandiose pillars that lined the front porch.

"It's not a mansion," Queenie protested. "Mansions have like fifty bedrooms."

"How many bedrooms do you have?"

Queenie held her hand up and counted. "One, two, four . . . eight, I think. Yeah, eight."

"Eight bedrooms?"

"Well, ten actually. If you count the two-bedroom guesthouse in the back."

Pudge was speechless.

"What?" Queenie asked innocently as she removed the keys from the ignition. "It's not like we have a butler or anything." She opened the driver-side door. "Are you coming inside or are you just going to sit there and stare?"

Pudge quickly unlocked her seatbelt and jumped out of the car. She grabbed a black garbage bag full of clothes from the backseat and began to stride toward the front door. Right before she stepped onto the porch, she came to a standstill. Queenie almost bumped into her from behind.

"What's wrong?" Queenie asked.

Pudge played with the bag in her hands. "What if your parents don't like me?" she asked. "What if they look at me funny? What if they don't want me here?"

"They're not going to look at you funny, I promise. I already told them all about you. They're excited to meet you. I bet my mom is already foaming at the mouth right now at the thought of taking you shopping."

"Why does everyone in your family want to take me shopping?"

Queenie laughed. "I don't know, I guess it's in our blood or something. McBrides just love any excuse to spend money, and shopping is the best way to do it."

"Are you sure it's okay with them that I'm here?"

"Yes. Will you stop worrying so much? My parents may be a little uptight about certain things, but not about this. They wanted you to come and spend the holiday with us. I'm sure they are going to love you." Queenie hit Pudge in the side with her hip and nudged her forward. "Come on. Let's go inside before I change my mind."

As soon as they entered the foyer, Pudge dropped the garbage bag onto the coffee-colored hardwood floors and looked around in awe. The ceilings stretched high into the air and a crystal chandelier hung over their heads. Three large vases sat in the corner of the room, each holding luscious bouquets of red, orange and yellow mums.

"I was wondering when you'd come inside," a woman screeched, as she came galloping into the foyer. She was dressed in tan slacks and a white blouse, with a ceramic orange leaf pin on the breast pocket. Her hair was done up as if she had just gotten back from the hair salon, and she wore bright red lipstick. "I was watching you from the kitchen window," she confessed, planting a kiss on the side of Queenie's cheek. It left a red smudge in its wake.

When Pudge pointed to it and giggled, Queenie rushed to wipe it off with the back of her hand. Then she handled the formalities like a pro. "Hey, Mom. This is the girl I've been telling you about. Everyone calls her Pudge."

The woman clapped her hands together and turned her attention to Pudge. "Hello dear," she cooed. "Welcome to our home."

"Hello ma'am," Pudge said, just like she had practiced in the car, and extended her hand.

"Oh, please, call me Carol," Queenie's mother said with an empathetic smile. She shooed Pudge's hand away and gathered her up in her arms, as if Pudge were a starving child from the Sudan. Then she stepped back and held onto Pudge's shoulders. "My heart nearly snapped in two when Queenie told me what happened to you," she said. "Queenie has been a thorn in our sides at times, and she's pulled quite the stunt or two before, but we would never, ever think of kicking her out of our home."

"Dad might disagree with you," Queenie joked. "If I had gotten thrown out of Sampson Academy like all of the other schools, I don't know what he would have done."

"We're just glad you finally grew out of that phase," her mom returned. "Now, why don't you show our houseguest to her room so she can get washed up for supper? Your sister and brother-in-law are flying in later tonight so they'll be here bright and early tomorrow for Thanksgiving." She looked back at Pudge and pinched her cheek with enthusiasm. "And on Friday we can wake up early and go shopping! I know where to go for all the best Thanksgiving deals. We can get you a whole new wardrobe!"

Queenie immediately grabbed hold of Pudge's sleeve and dragged her away before her mother could get in another hug.

"Wow," said Pudge as they walked down the hallway and up the stairs to the second floor of the house. "Is she always so cheerful?"

"Yes, especially when we have company. For some reason, she loves playing hostess. Just be glad she didn't grab hold of your cheeks. JJ's cheeks used to hurt for days from getting pinched so much while she was here."

When Pudge brushed her hand along the side of her face, Queenie began to laugh. "Don't worry," she said. "I think your cheeks are safe." They reached the stair landing, and Queenie took a sharp turn to the right.

"She seems really nice and everything," said Pudge, following close behind. "Do you get along?"

"For the most part, we do. I'll be honest—she wasn't too thrilled when I first came out of the closet. But that's partly because she caught me kissing the maid."

"What?!"

"Never mind. It's kind of a crazy story. But we get along a lot better now because she accepts me for me. It probably helped that I stopped being such a jerk to her and my father."

"Why were you a jerk?"

"I don't really know," Queenie admitted. "My parents and I see the world very differently. But I know they care about me and that's all that matters."

After a couple of turns, Queenie stopped in front of a bedroom door down the hall and on the left. "Your room, Miss," she said in a fake butler's voice and swept her hand in front of the doorway. "As you can see, there are fresh towels and washcloths on your bed. You also have your own private bathroom. Dinner will be served promptly at six."

"Shut up," Pudge said with a silly grin, and pushed Queenie aside.

"I'll see you downstairs in half an hour." Queenie turned to go, then paused and added, "One thing you should know—my mother doesn't like it when we're late for dinner."

"Wait," said Pudge, sticking her head back out in the hallway. "Where's your bedroom."

"Down this way, fourth door on the right."

"Fourth door on the right," Pudge repeated to herself as she gently closed the door behind her. She paused, her eyes soaking up every inch of the guestroom. Then she ran full force at the four-poster bed and leapt onto the mattress, rolling over on her back and cradling her head in her hands.

"How in the world did I get so lucky?" she asked aloud as she gazed up at the ceiling.

When it was Thanksgiving at her house, she would always give thanks for all of the good things in her life at the dinner table right before her father carved the turkey. Even though she wasn't sitting at the dinner table with her hands folded over the empty plate in front of her, she closed her eyes and whispered, "God or whatever is out there—thanks for taking care of me. Thanks for Queenie. Thanks giving me a place to stay. And thanks for always looking out for me. I know you love me just the way that I am, because you never make mistakes. I just wish my parents could see that, too."

When the doorbell rang late Thanksgiving morning, Kendal expected to see a few of her relatives standing on the front step with open arms, ready to take part in all of the holiday hoopla. But when she opened the door, it was JJ standing there with an apologetic look on her face. She looked like the same old JJ, wearing a backpack over the shoulder of her blue jacket and holding it tightly to her side.

"Uh, hi," Kendal said awkwardly.

"I'm sorry to show up like this without calling," JJ said quickly. "But I have a little something for you and I knew that we would both be home for Thanksgiving break. So, I figured I'd drop by and give it to you myself."

"Come in," Kendal replied.

"I promise I won't be long," said JJ, as she stepped inside. "I don't want to bother you."

"You aren't bothering me at all," said Kendal. "My mom and grandmother are inside cooking, and my dad is on the couch watching football. We were just waiting for my aunt and uncle and cousins to get here. Why don't you stay for a little bit and say hello to my parents?"

JJ shifted uncomfortably. "I don't know if that's such a good idea," she said. "I really just stopped by to give you this."

She pulled a black Nike shoebox out from the backpack.

"You came by to give me a pair of sneakers?"

"No," JJ laughed. "It's not a pair of sneakers. But I think you'll like what's actually inside."

"Can I open it now?" Kendal asked, lifting up the top of the box to take a peek. "You know how curious I can be."

JJ quickly slid her hand over the box to keep Kendal from opening it. "I'd prefer that you opened it when I wasn't standing right in front of you."

"Why?"

"You'll understand once you see it." JJ zipped up the empty backpack and flung it over her shoulder. "I know you're going to be busy over the Thanksgiving holiday and everything. But I'd really like to know what you think of it. Give me a call after you open it."

"You know I'm going to open the box as soon as you walk out the door. I'll probably give you a call later tonight. Are you going to be home, or are you going over to Queenie's?"

"Trust me. Queenie's already got a full house. She dropped me off at my house yesterday, so I'll probably just stay home with my parents for the rest of Thanksgiving break. I haven't seen them since I left for college, so I'm actually looking forward to hanging out with them."

"I know what you mean," said Kendal. "It's kind of funny how that happens. You can't wait to leave home, but then when you do you only end up missing everything about it— including your parents."

"Exactly." JJ let her hands hang awkwardly at her sides, not sure where to put them. "I should probably get going," she said, leaning forward to give Kendal a quick hug. "Tell your mom and dad that I said hello."

"I will. Tell your parents the same for me."

Kendal held the shoebox against her hip as she watched JJ make her way down the driveway and into her car. As soon as she drove away, Kendal closed the front door and raced up the stairs and into her bedroom. She crawled on top of her bed and set the shoebox down next to her. It took her less than a second to pry it open. Inside she found a thick stack of paper held together by a red ribbon. There was a pink Post-It note attached to the first page, and Kendal quickly recognized JJ's familiar scrawl. She gently plucked out the note and began to read:

Kendal,
  You once said, "The way we got together was like something right out of a novel." I couldn't agree more. That's why I wrote "our" story for my writing class. I had been struggling with a bad case of writer's block at the beginning of the semester. Then Queenie told me to "write what I know." So I stopped trying to write about things that I knew nothing about, and I wrote about our experience instead. I don't have a title for it yet, but I'm thinking about calling it "The Trouble with Emily Dickinson" or something like that. Let me know what you think. I have to hand the original in when we get back from Thanksgiving break. But this is your copy to keep. No matter what happens between us from here on out, you'll always have something to remind you of our senior year at Sampson Academy.
  Love always,
  JJ

Kendal felt a familiar tingling inside of her that she hadn't felt in quite some time. She smiled to herself as she carefully lifted the stack of papers out of the shoebox and slowly untied the ribbon. Then she fell onto her stomach and began to read. She read page after page without pause, as if she had just unearthed a secret treasure. When her mom finally called her downstairs for dinner, Kendal could hardly believe that she had been lying there reading for almost three hours. It felt as though she had been sucked in to some kind of time warp.

Kendal reluctantly set what was left of the stack aside and marked her place with the ribbon. After dinner, she'd planned to help with the dishes and sneak away to finish the rest. Even though she knew how it was going to end, she couldn't wait to read the rest. JJ had captured every thing about their story so perfectly that she wanted to relive every moment, every nervous glance, and every electric tingle all over again—even if only on paper.

JJ shoveled more turkey and mashed potatoes into her mouth, despite the fact that her stomach felt as if it were going to explode. When her mom set the pumpkin pie down in the center of the dining room table, she groaned.

"What? I thought you loved my pumpkin pie?"

"I do, I'm just too full right now to eat anything else."

The phone rang in the kitchen and JJ assumed it was Queenie calling to regale her with tall tales from the McBride family Thanksgiving feast. She had been wondering how Pudge felt around Queenie's parents, especially her mother. Whenever JJ went with Queenie to visit her parents, her mother would fawn all over JJ as if she were some charity project. She knew that Queenie's mother meant well, but it still made JJ uncomfortable whenever she pinched her cheeks. In fact, her cheeks hurt just thinking about it.

She excused herself from the table and picked up the phone in the kitchen. "I'm glad you called the house phone," she said while hopping up on the counter next to the sink. "I have no idea what I did with my cell phone. I think it's stuffed in the bottom of my duffle bag somewhere."

"So that's the reason why you weren't answering," Kendal

answered. "I tried calling your cell phone and it went straight to voicemail, so I thought I'd try your parents' number instead."

"Kendal?" JJ stammered. "Did you finish it already?"

"I couldn't put it down. I read half of it before dinner, and then I ate really fast so that I could help clean up and finish the rest." Her laughter reached through the phone, delighting JJ's ears. "My parents thought I was avoiding them for the whole day."

"What did you think?" JJ asked. "And be honest. I'm going to be graded on it."

"I think," Kendal paused, working to find the right words. "I think . . . that it's incredible, JJ. Aside from changing our names, you captured everything that happened so well, I felt like I was reliving it all over again as I read. You reminded me of the reason why I fell in love with you. It made me miss you and us a lot."

"I know what you mean. That's how I felt when I was writing it. Do you think it's realistic enough? It's not cheesy or anything, is it?"

"Cheesy?"

"You know what I mean."

"No," said Kendal. "It's definitely not cheesy. I'm no writing expert or anything, but I think you're going to get a really good grade on it."

"I hope my professor likes it, too. She told me that if she thinks the novel is good enough, she's going to try and help me get it published. She has a good friend who works at a publishing company in New York."

"That's great!"

JJ rubbed her full stomach and sighed. "I'm really glad you liked it. I kind of wrote it for you—well, for us—so I was nervous about your feedback."

"I loved it," said Kendal. "Honestly, it gave me some closure."

"Me, too."

"I don't know why, but I feel like I can move on now without any regrets. We had something special, and it will always remain special, no matter what happens between us."

"That's right," said JJ. "And when I become a big famous author, you can tell everyone that you dated me back in the day."

"Forget that. If you become a big famous author, I want a small percentage of your book sales. Without me, you wouldn't even have a story."

"You were always so demanding," JJ teased.

"And you were always a pushover."

"Hey!" JJ yelled lightheartedly and jumped off the counter.

"You know I'm only teasing you," said Kendal. She held the phone aside to answer her mother, who was calling for her in the background. "Hey, my mom wants me to come spend time with the rest of the family since I spent the day reading alone in my room. I should go."

"Okay. I need to help my parents clean up the table anyway."

"Thanks again for the gift. I love it. I'll cherish it always."

"I couldn't have written it without you."

"Maybe I'll see you when we're home for Christmas break?"

"Yeah," said JJ. "I'd like that. Talk to you later." A few seconds after she hung up her phone, it rang again and JJ answered it immediately. "Did you forget to tell me how wonderful I am or something?"

"What are you talking about?" Queenie asked on the other end.

"Oh—I thought you were—never mind. How's the McBride family Thanksgiving feast going this year?"

"Absolutely splendidly. My mother is fawning all over Pudge just like I thought she would."

"What about your father?"

"He pulled me into his study after dinner to give me a little lecture on responsibility, like making sure Pudge goes to school, does her homework, has a curfew—all that stuff. But then he did something really shocking. He told me he was proud of me for doing something so selfless, and that he was glad I had finally grown up."

"Wow."

"He never says stuff like that. But that's not even the best part. He also asked if I needed some extra money since Pudge is going to be living with me. I told him that I was going to get a part-time job to help pay for things instead. You should have seen his face! I thought he was going to faint right where he was standing."

"Sounds like it's all working out just like you had planned."

"It's going better than I anticipated, that's for sure. How's the Jenkins family Thanksgiving feast going this year?"

"It's kind of boring actually. My older brother didn't end up coming home, so it's just my parents and me."

"At least that leaves more food for you."

"Speaking of food, I've finally digested enough so I can sink my teeth into my mom's pumpkin pie. I'll call you tomorrow, okay?"

JJ hung up the phone again and walked back into the dining room with an additional hop to her step.

"Who was on the phone?" her mother asked.

"Kendal. Well, she called first. That last phone call was Queenie."

"I thought you and Kendal were just friends?"

"We are." JJ pulled her chair up to the table. She reached out for a slice of pumpkin pie and scooped up a piece with her fork.

"And how's Queenie?"

"She's good," JJ replied before taking a bite. "In fact, she's better than good. She's the new and improved I-Queenie 4000, and she's ready to take on the world."

CHAPTER 28

Pudge grimaced as she picked up the last shopping bag from the car with her left thumb. Her arms and hands were full of bags of designer clothes that Queenie's mother had bought for her when they were home over Thanksgiving break. She even had one bag dangling from her teeth.

"Do you need some help with those?" Queenie asked with a playful smile. She reached out and snagged the bag hanging from Pudge's mouth. "You look like you're going to fall over."

"I still can't believe that your mom bought me all this stuff. I have more clothes than I've ever had in my entire life."

"Good," said Queenie. She pinched her own nose, "It's about time you got rid of that dirty gray sweatshirt that you wear all of the time. It smells like a five-week-old wet sock."

"But it's my favorite sweatshirt," Pudge argued, as she sniffed at her sleeve.

JJ returned to the parking garage at that moment to help them carry the rest of the bags up to the apartment. "Why are you trying to carry all of that by yourself?" she asked as soon as she saw Pudge standing there like a whimpering puppy as she struggled to balance all of the bags in her arms and hands. JJ took a few of the bags. "What is all this stuff anyway?"

"Clothes," said Pudge. "Queenie's mom bought them for me. She said I needed a brand new wardrobe to start off on the right foot."

JJ laughed. "That's sounds like something Queenie's mom would say."

"She was right," said Queenie. "A new wardrobe can make all the difference in the world." She leaned over to Pudge. "JJ could use one herself."

"Shut it," said JJ. "My clothes are just fine."

"If you say so," said Queenie, as she kicked the driver's door closed with her heel and pressed the lock button on her keychain. "Well, ladies. I'd say that our little Thanksgiving adventure was just what we all needed. Pudge got to meet my parents, I got to relax a bit, and JJ—" she paused and tossed her head to the side. "What did you get out of it besides a bag full of leftover turkey?"

"Me?" JJ shrugged her shoulders. "I guess I finally got some closure with Kendal."

"Closure?" Queenie asked skeptically. "Does anyone really ever get closure when it comes to relationships? It's such an elusive concept."

"What's closure?" asked Pudge.

"It's just another word for moving on," JJ told her.

"Actually, it's just another word for, 'I know I'm not over you but I'm going to suck it up and try to move on anyway'," said Queenie.

Pudge looked confused.

"Are you sure you want her to be your legal guardian?" JJ asked. "You still have time to back out."

"I'm just being honest," said Queenie. "There's no such thing as closure."

"Whatever," JJ sighed. "All I know is that I'm finally okay with Kendal and me being friends."

"So that means you're single and ready to mingle?" Pudge asked.

JJ shot her a look.

"She got that from me," Queenie whispered.

"Figures," said JJ. She turned to Pudge. "Single, yes. Ready to mingle, no. I'm going to spend some much-needed time with myself for a little while."

"But at least she's finally changed her relationship status on Facebook," Queenie said patting JJ's shoulder with her free hand.

They reached the elevator and rode it up to the apartment. As soon as they were inside, Pudge tossed all of the shopping bags she had been holding onto the floor next to the luggage.

"What time is your presentation tomorrow?" JJ asked, flopping down on the couch.

"Class starts at quarter after eight," said Queenie. "Probably sometime shortly after that. Why?"

"I don't have to hand in my novel project until eleven, and I want to come and see you and Pudge in action."

"Be prepared to be dazzled," Queenie said, wiggling her fingers in the air. "Pudge is going to be amazing, but only if she ditches her ratty gray sweatshirt beforehand."

"You don't have to worry about my stinky sweatshirt," said Pudge, punching Queenie lightly in the shoulder. "I'm going to wear some of my new clothes instead."

"Are you nervous at all?" JJ asked.

"No," said Queenie. "It'll be a piece of cake."

"I was talking to Pudge."

Pudge hesitated as she nervously fiddled with her hands, "A little bit. I don't want to mess up."

"You aren't going to mess up," said Queenie. "Just do exactly what we practiced, and you'll be fine."

"Let's stop talking about it, okay?" Pudge picked up a few of the shopping bags off the floor. "Should I put these clothes in your closet for now?"

"Yeah," said Queenie. "Once JJ leaves for Smith, you'll have your own room and your own closet for all of your new stuff."

Once Pudge had gathered up the bags and left to lug them down the hallway and into Queenie's bedroom, JJ turned to Queenie. "You sure she's up to this? It's kind of a lot of pressure to put on her, especially with everything she's been through lately."

"What pressure?" Queenie asked. "She's not the one getting the grade. I am."

"Exactly. She's probably afraid of letting you down or something. Besides, it's not easy to get up in front of a crowd of strangers and bare your soul like that. I should know. It's the reason I used to have stage fright."

"Do you think I made a mistake?"

"I don't know," said JJ. "I wouldn't want her to freak out or anything. Not everyone is as laid back as you are when it comes to public speaking, you know. Look at her history. She has a pattern of running away from stressful situations. What would keep her from running away from this, too?"

Queenie didn't respond. Instead she kept her eyes planted on the hallway. The entire time she had been working on her sociology project, she had thought that it would be in Pudge's best interest to be a part of it. Now, she began to wonder if that was really the case after all.

As soon as the alarm sounded, Queenie hit the snooze button and pulled the blanket up over her head. Less than a second later, she bolted upright on the couch with an uneasy feeling in her stomach. She listened for the sound of the shower, but there was no running water. She leaned forward and looked in the kitchen, but there was no one was sitting at the table eating breakfast. After a moment, she picked up her cell phone and checked the time. It was after seven, and Pudge should have been up by now.

Queenie fell frantically off the couch and darted into her bedroom. "Unbelievable!" she yelled as soon as she saw the empty bed. She picked up a pillow and threw it across the room. "She did it again!"

"Who did what?" JJ asked, popping her head in the doorway while rubbing at her eyes.

"Pudge," Queenie stated. "She ran away again."

"Are you sure?"

"No, but the bed is empty and she's not anywhere else in the apartment. Where else could she have gone? We were supposed to walk to the university together." Queenie sat down on the bed and flopped onto her back. "You must have been right, JJ. The stress of helping me with the project was too much for her. She must have run away to get out if it."

"Maybe she dropped by the shelter first," said JJ. "Why don't you call Izzy?"

"Izzy isn't going to the shelter this morning. She's going straight to the university to watch the presentation."

"You can still call the shelter, though."

"I'm not wasting my time." Queenie got up and grabbed her bathrobe off the chair in the corner of the room. "I have to shower and get ready for class."

"You're not even going to look for her?"

"I'm tired of her running away from me. And this time, I'm not going to chase her."

"Yeah, but—"

"JJ, this has seriously got to stop," said Queenie. "Pudge can't live with me if she is always going to run away when things get tough. I won't be able to handle that. I'll make sure to tell Professor Duncan what happened as soon as I get to school. And after my presentation is finished, I'll deal with finding Pudge. But right now, I've got to put myself first."

"I understand," said JJ.

* * *

When they arrived at the classroom door, Izzy was already there. She was sitting in the front row, dressed in a black skirt and a light-pink blouse with a black cardigan sweater wrapped around her shoulders. She waved to them and pointed to an empty seat next to her.

"Go and sit with her," Queenie said to JJ. "I've got to catch Professor Duncan before he leaves his office and let him know what's going on."

"Do you want me to tell Izzy what happened?" asked JJ. "She'll probably want to know what's going on when she doesn't see Pudge standing next to you."

Queenie nodded quickly and rushed down the hall. She knocked hard on Professor Duncan's door, ready to break the bad news.

"Queenie," he said when he opened the door, "is everything all set? You look like you're in a bit of a panic."

"I am," Queenie began. "There's a little hiccup with the original plan."

"Really?" Professor Duncan asked. "Pudge didn't say anything about that. In fact, she was so excited about the presentation that she got here an hour early."

Queenie's mouth open and closed. "She did what?"

"She came here early. I saw her standing outside of the classroom door when I arrived, so I let her relax for a little while in my office." He opened the door wide enough so that Queenie could see Pudge sitting in one of the chairs in front of his desk.

"I thought—" Queenie shook the words from her mouth and stared directly at Pudge. "You've been here the whole time?"

"What did you think?" Pudge asked, rising from her seat confidently. "That I ran away or something?"

"Maybe," said Queenie. "Why didn't you just tell me where you were going?"

"You were still asleep," said Pudge. "And I didn't want to wake you. I couldn't sleep at all last night because I was so nervous. As soon as the sun came up, I got up, got dressed and came straight here."

"I'm impressed," said Queenie.

"So I am," Professor Duncan added. "Looks like you've both been good influences on each other." He checked his watch. "Almost time to start class. Are you girls ready?"

"Ready as we'll ever be," said Queenie.

They left the office together and followed Professor Duncan down the hall.

"Why do you keep looking at me like that?" Pudge asked Queenie, who had been glancing at her out of the corner of her eyes.

"I've never seen you like this before." She pointed at Pudge's hair, which had been brushed and styled so that it hung delicately just above her shoulders. "Look at your hair. You're even wearing a skirt!"

Pudge held onto the light-blue fabric of the skirt and smiled. "I like wearing skirts. Your mom bought this one for me and I wanted to wear it today."

"You clean up real nice," said Queenie. "I got so used to seeing you in a sweatshirt and jeans with your hair in tangles that you caught me by surprise. I almost didn't recognize you at first."

"It feels nice to be able to get cleaned up," said Pudge.

They reached the entrance to the classroom and looked on as Professor Duncan walked in ahead of them to address the class. Pudge gulped hard.

"This is your last chance to turn and run," Queenie whispered. "But if you do, I'm not going to chase after you anymore."

"I'm not going anywhere," said Pudge. "A good friend of

mine once told me that running away doesn't solve anything, because wherever you go your problems are going to follow you. The only thing running away does is change the scenery."

Queenie smiled. "Sounds like a really smart friend."

"Eh, she's all right." Pudge grinned. "But I agree with her. I think maybe I'll stick around this time and see what happens. Besides, I don't mind the scenery so much."

Pudge helped with the power point of the presentation while Queenie delivered the jarring statistics associated with LGBT teen homelessness. Once the presentation ended, Queenie walked to the center of the lecture hall floor and addressed the class.

"Showing statistics and going over pertinent information about LGBT teen homelessness is a great way to give you a sense of how important this sociological issue really is," she said, as her voice carried throughout the lecture hall. "But statistics can only do so much. They can't show you how it feels to be a homeless teen, struggling with your sexuality. They can't show you what it's like to live on the streets and wonder where you are going to sleep at night or where your next meal is coming from. And they certainly can't show the pain and hopelessness LGBT teens feel when they are kicked out of their own homes, by their very own parents, for something they have no control over."

Queenie held out her hand and turned to Pudge. "But, thankfully, I was prepared and brought more than just a power point display of statistics with me this morning."

Pudge stepped down off the podium, where she had been standing, and joined Queenie at the center of the lecture hall. The faces in the crowd melted into one colorful blur as she swallowed a generous gulp of air.

"Most of my friends call me Pudge," she began nervously, "But my real name is Margaret O'Sullivan. At the beginning of last summer, I finally got up enough courage to tell my parents that I was gay. I'm an only child, so I figured they'd be more understanding or something . . . ."

She stopped, losing her place. With a panicked expression, she looked at Queenie who urged her to keep going. "Um," Pudge took a quick breath and continued, "I've always known that something was different about me. I used to have crushes on some of my friends at school and I didn't understand why. After I talked with my school counselor, she suggested that I join the gay-straight alliance group. That's when I realized that I was gay. They made me feel comfortable enough to talk about things, and some of the members had already told their own parents and it was no big deal. But when I told mine, it was a big deal. My dad said I couldn't live there anymore and my mom didn't say anything at all. So I grabbed some clothes and I left. I spent the next three months on the streets and I made some friends with other kids who had run away. Every once and a while we would go to the homeless shelter on Boylston Street. And when it got colder, we'd stay there more often. Everyone at the shelter is really nice. They gave us meals and cots to sleep on. They even have activities and stuff to keep us busy."

Pudge spotted Izzy and JJ sitting in the front row and instantly felt her body relax. "They even helped some of my friends find new places to live. Others weren't so lucky. I know some kids who have gotten arrested, gotten into drugs and even prostitution. Some have even committed suicide. They had nowhere else to turn so they just gave up. I could have ended up just like them if I hadn't met Queenie. Even though I could have gone into foster care or a group home, I didn't want to. Some of us don't want to do that because we don't feel comfortable. Some of us really just want our parents to let us come home. I tried to go home. I even went back on Halloween to ask if I could. But my parents didn't want me to live there if I was still gay. And I just can't stop being gay."

As hard as she tried, Pudge couldn't keep herself from crying. "It really hurts a lot when your own parents don't accept who you are, especially when you can't do anything about it. But I'm lucky because now I have people in my life who do care about me and accept me and love me just the way I am. Queenie has not only given me a place to stay, she also gave me her friendship and I truly believe her friendship saved my life. After I went to see my parents on Halloween, I don't know what I would have done if Queenie hadn't been there. I was so upset, I could have, I might have—well, let's just say that I'm glad she was there."

Pudge sighed heavily and wiped her eyes with her hands. "There are so many kids out there who are just like me. Only, they don't have someone like Queenie in their lives. She took the time to reach out to me and to show me that I mattered. That's really all we want. Just for someone to tell us that we matter, since our own parents can't or won't, for whatever reason. One month ago, I was a homeless gay teen. I was a statistic. But because there are people in my life who care enough to do something about this issue, I'm not just a statistic anymore. I have a place to live again. But more importantly, I have a family again."

As soon as Pudge finished speaking, the student audience erupted into applause, most wiping tears from their eyes and many even standing up from their seats. Professor Duncan smiled at Queenie like a proud parent whose child had gone from straight D's to straight A's, while JJ gave a slight fist pump in her direction. Izzy leapt up from her seat to give Pudge a hug.

"Margaret?" Queenie asked as she made her way over to them and joined in the embrace. "That's your real name? That's the big classified secret?"

"I hate it," said Pudge.

"Why? It's such a beautiful name. I think you should use it more often."

"Forget about my name! How did I do?"

"You did an incredible job," said Queenie. "I can't thank you enough for putting yourself out there like that."

"She's right," Izzy added. "You were amazing. I'm so proud of you."

"I've never done anything like that before in my whole life," said Pudge. "It was kind of cool."

"I hope you're ready to do it again this afternoon," said Professor Duncan. "Because my next class starts at one."

CHAPTER 29

On an overcast and brooding snowy day in January, Queenie and Izzy were finally able to meet for their long-awaited official first date. Between exams and Christmas break, their schedules never matched up. But as soon as Queenie returned to the city for her spring semester at Boston University, she called Izzy and asked her to go for a walk.

They met in the middle of Boston Common, despite the impending snowstorm. Izzy was wrapped warmly in a gray wool winter coat, with a black hat and black mittens. Queenie wore a red scarf over her black leather jacket. Her ears were bright pink because she had forgotten to grab a hat for herself.

"Your first semester at college is in the books," said Izzy as they strolled along the snow-covered sidewalk. "Was it everything you expected?"

"Not at all," Queenie said with a slight laugh. "But that's the best part. Un-expectations make life worth living."

"Un-expectations? I don't think that's a real word."

"It's not," said Queenie. "I just made it up."

Snow continued to fall softly around them, covering the ground like a cozy white blanket.

"What did you end up getting on your project?" Izzy asked.

"What do you think?"

"An A?"

"Hardest A I ever had to work for in my life," said Queenie. "But it was definitely worth it. I even signed up for another one of Professor Duncan's classes this semester. I hate to admit it, but he grew on me."

"I think that everyone connects with at least one professor during college in a way that they don't with others," said Izzy. "My favorite was my psychology professor. She helped me realize a lot of things about myself, feelings and stuff I was still holding on to from being homeless."

Queenie could feel the snowflakes as they landed on her head and melted into her hair. "I didn't think Professor Duncan was all that great when we first met. But he turned out to be a pretty cool guy after all."

"First impressions can be deceiving," said Izzy. "I didn't think you were all that great when we first met. But you turned out to be a pretty cool girl yourself."

"I knew once you got to know me, you'd eventually come around," Queenie said smartly.

"Oh, really?" said Izzy.

They walked in silence for a moment, watching everything around them turn white with snow.

"How did the rest of your semester go?" Queenie asked finally.

"I'm still maintaining straight A's," said Izzy. She reached out with her mitten and caught a snowflake in her palm. "One more semester and then the real world begins."

"Think you can put up with me when I'm still in college mode and you're in the real world?' "

"I'm certainly going to try. Don't take this the wrong way or anything—my friends thought I was crazy when I told them I was dating a freshman."

"Yeah, but did you tell them that I'm a lot more mature than the average freshman?"

"Nope."

"What did you tell them?"

"I told them I wasn't crazy. I was just in love."

"I like that response better."

Izzy reached up and hooked her arm through Queenie's. "So, where are we going exactly?" She looked up and down, pretending to search the street. "Is a limousine going to swing around the corner, pick us up and take us some place fancy?"

"Not this time," Queenie answered smoothly. "I'm done with limos. I have something a bit less ostentatious planned." She led Izzy along the footpath and into a wider area where a few remaining food vendors were staked out, braving the cold. "I think I brought just enough money with me for a hot dog or two," she smiled, leaving Izzy standing off to the side.

She returned shortly, carrying two steaming hotdogs with all the trimmings. "I believe you once said that your idea of the perfect date was sitting on the grass at Boston Common, eating hotdogs and looking up at the stars," Queenie stated, handing one of the hotdogs over to Izzy.

"Sitting on the grass is out of the question," Izzy replied. "And the only thing we'll be able to see when we look up is the snow falling down on us. But the hotdogs are perfect."

"Tell me the truth," Queenie asked with her mouth full and a streak of mustard smeared across her lips, "Are you impressed or what?"

Izzy laughed as she handed Queenie a napkin. "Tremendously," she said. "I couldn't ask for anything better."

"Aren't you glad you waited around to give me another chance?"

"Ask me again in six months," Izzy teased. "Then we'll talk."

Pudge sat on the floor in front of the television with an American history textbook open next to her. She purposely neglected the book and flipped through the television stations with the remote control. Queenie walked into the living room, took in the scene before her and smiled to herself. She casually walked by Pudge and snatched the remote control right out of her hands, turning off the television in the process.

"Hey!" Pudge yelled. "I was watching that."

"I know," said Queenie. "That's why I turned it off." She eyed the open textbook on the floor. "You should be reading about the Civil War instead of watching reruns of *Jersey Shore*. One is more educational and intellectually stimulating than the other, and I don't think I have to tell you which one is which."

Pudge groaned and pulled the textbook closer to her. "I hate homework," she mumbled.

"Me, too," said Queenie. "But I still do it. Besides, we made a pact. You promised me that you would do your homework as soon as you got home from school. It's my responsibility to make sure you live up to your promise."

"But I feel so far behind," said Pudge. "Everyone in my class knows this stuff already."

"What do you expect? You missed the entire fall semester of ninth grade. You are behind, but now you have a chance to catch up. I'm here to help you. Ask me anything."

Pudge nodded and scanned the pages of the book. "Okay, who was in charge of the first all-Black 54th Boston Regiment in the Union?" She looked up at Queenie. "You should know this, because you live in Boston."

Queenie paused, holding her finger to her chin. Finally she sighed and said, "It's been a while since I was in the ninth grade. Let me see that book."

Pudge laughed. "Some help you are. The answer is Robert Gould Shaw."

"Whatever," said Queenie. "Finish your reading assignment

and then we can go pick out a new paint color for your bedroom walls. Once JJ is gone, you can move into her room for good."

"When does JJ leave for Smith?"

"I'm helping her pack up the U-Haul tomorrow. Then Izzy and I are going to meet her at her dorm room and help her get settled."

"Can I come, too?" Pudge asked.

"No, you can't. There's that little thing called school that's more important."

"But I want to say goodbye to JJ before she leaves."

"You can say goodbye to her tonight," said Queenie. "She'll be home later. Right now, you have a homework assignment to finish." She pointed at the book with a stern finger.

"All right, all right," said Pudge. "Geez, you're just like my mother!"

"Be thankful for that," Queenie said as she sat back on the couch and tucked her hands behind her head.

"Just wait until I start dating," Pudge joked. "You'll be in trouble then."

Queenie grinned. "I think I can handle it."

* * *

"Are you sure that this is all of your stuff?" Queenie asked, tossing a black duffle bag into the back of the U-Haul. "There's nothing else left in the apartment?"

"This is everything I own," said JJ, stuffing the box she had been holding into a tiny open space in the corner. "Hurry up and close up the truck before it all falls out."

Queenie reached up and pulled down the latch to the trailer door. "Told you we wouldn't be able to fit all of your stuff in the back of my BMW."

"You know, I'm really going to miss the fact that you're right all of the time," said JJ. "And how you love to throw it in my face whenever you have the chance."

"And I'm sure going to miss your side-splitting sense of humor," Queenie responded on cue.

They wrestled good-naturedly with one another before Queenie gave JJ one last push and messed up her hair. "Seriously," Queenie said. "I'm going to have to teach Pudge how to engage in some friendly, witty banter or else I'm going to go nuts."

"Don't you mean, Margaret?"

"Whatever. She'll always be 'Pudge' to me."

"I'm sure that *Margaret* can hold her own." JJ opened the driver's side door of the U-Haul truck and tossed her backpack onto the passenger seat. "She's pretty witty herself."

"Witty banter or not, I hope she likes living with me."

"Are you kidding? She's going to love having you as a roommate. Did you see the way she was ogling my room? She couldn't wait to move in there."

"It's been a while since she's had a room of her own," said Queenie. "Can you blame her for being excited? Besides, she's going to miss you."

"I'm going to miss her, too," said JJ. "And I'm glad that things worked out this way. With me going to Smith, there's plenty of room for Pudge. It was meant to be. It's like I always say, everything happens for a reason."

"I'm beginning to think your 'everything-happens-for-a-reason' outlook isn't as crazy as I thought."

"So the plan is for you and Izzy to meet me at my dorm so you can help me unpack, right?"

"Yes," Queenie confirmed. "As soon as I go pick her up, we'll be on our way."

"Good. Otherwise it would take me all day to unpack

this stuff and carry it up to my dorm room."

"I can't believe you're going live in a dorm again," said Queenie. "After four years at Sampson, you couldn't pay me to do it. I need my own space."

"I'd love to have my own space," said JJ. She lifted herself up into the driver's seat of the U-Haul. "But I can't afford an apartment right now."

"Neither can I. That's exactly why my parents are paying my rent."

"You can make me feel better by telling me how much you appreciate that fact now."

"Are you kidding?" said Queenie as she held onto the driver's side door. "I've told them 'thank you' more times in the past three months than I have throughout my entire adolescence. I'm forever a changed woman."

"I'm proud of you," JJ told her. "I want you to know that."

"Let's not get too sentimental here," Queenie said, looking away. "You know I don't like all that emotional stuff."

"I'm serious," said JJ. "I was really worried about you at the beginning of the semester. But you've really changed, Queenie."

"Well," Queenie sighed, "I'm proud of you, too. You're an independent woman making your own decisions. That has to feel good."

"It does."

"Just make sure you keep it up while you are at Smith. Don't let yourself get sidetracked when the next Kendal McCarthy comes along."

"I won't," said JJ. "I promise. Besides, she's one of a kind." She took a deep breath and fiddled with the steering wheel. "I'm really going to miss you a lot, Queenie."

"What did I just tell you about the sentimental stuff?"

"I can't help it. You know how I get."

"I know how *you* get," said Queenie. "But I don't want to start crying like a silly fool."

"One more sentimental comment and I promise I'm done," JJ replied. She buckled her seatbelt and returned her hands to the steering wheel. "I'm really sorry for underestimating you and for questioning your motives when it came to your project and volunteering at the shelter. I know that it hurt your feelings."

"You only underestimated me because I gave you a reason to," said Queenie. "I've always had ulterior motives. How could you have known that this would be any different?"

"I should have known because you're my best friend. I should have given you the benefit of the doubt."

"If it's any consolation, I underestimated you, too," Queenie reasoned. "I never thought you'd be able to manage the situation with Kendal the way that you did, or be as independent as you have been lately. So that makes us even."

"Maybe. I'm just really happy for the way things turned out for you. That project and everything that came out of it was incredible."

"Speaking of projects, what did you end up getting on yours?"

"Eh, I only got B-plus. My professor loved the story overall, but she said that my editing skills still need a lot of work."

"That sucks."

"Not really," said JJ. "She was right. My editing skills stink. But she also said that I should show it to my new writing professors at Smith, because they might be able to give me some additional feedback and help me revise it a little so that I can still try to get it published."

"There you go," said Queenie. "Who knows, maybe it will be a best-seller someday."

"I don't know about that. I bet your memoir would be a

best-seller, though."

"Oh, yeah? I thought you had no interest in writing it."

"Maybe I've changed my mind."

"Really?" Queenie asked, somewhat intrigued. "What would you call it?"

JJ slipped the key in the ignition and started up the truck. "I don't know," she said, weighing her thoughts. "Maybe 'The Education of Queenie McBride' or something lame like that."

Queenie repeated the title aloud. "It's not lame," she said. "I like it. I like it a lot. And I promise to give you plenty of juicy material for the forthcoming sequel." She leaned over and gave JJ a hug then stepped back and closed the door.

"When we say goodbye at Smith, I want to see some tears," said JJ.

"I make no guarantees."

JJ cracked a smile. "I'll see you later then," she said as she pulled away.

"Not if I see you first," Queenie called out.

She remained standing at the side of the curb with her eyes hitched to the back of the U-Haul, watching intently as it reached the end of the street and made a left at the corner stop sign before disappearing from view.

"And a whole new story begins," Queenie said out loud to no one. Then she smacked both of her hands together and rubbed them eagerly. "I can't wait to find out what happens next."

Meet **Lyndsey D'Arcangelo**

Lyndsey is an award-winning author and freelance writer from Buffalo, New York. She loves music, college basketball, baggy clothes, feel-good movies and the color blue. Basically, Lyndsey is an ordinary individual who strongly believes that she can positively impact the world through writing.

In her first novel, *The Trouble with Emily Dickinson*, she introduces JJ and Queenie as seniors in a private high school. Both girls struggle to discover who they really are and where their lives are headed. The book is available as an e-book and print book through Amazon.com.

For more about Lyndsey and her writing, visit her website:

www.LyndseyDarcangelo.com

Become a published author!

Lyndsey is collecting personal, real-life stories from high school students for her LGBT anthology, *My Story is Out: High School Years*. If your story is published, you will earn royalties.

To learn more about Lyndsey's story needs and story submission information, check out her website:

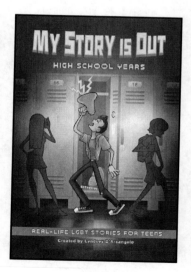

WALKER MEMORIAL LIBRARY
800 Main Street
Westbrook, ME 04092
207-854-0630

com

Do you have a great story to share?

OMG! My Reality! For Teens

Publishing Syndicate is now accepting stories for our new teen anthology series!

This new anthology will feature a collection of personal real-life stories written by and about teens. We are looking for humorous, heart-warming and inspiring stories **written by individuals 25 years and younger about teen life.**

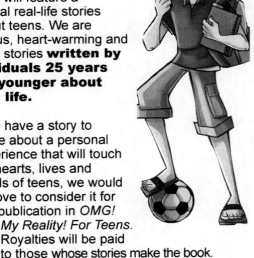

If you have a story to share about a personal experience that will touch the hearts, lives and souls of teens, we would love to consider it for publication in *OMG! My Reality! For Teens*. Royalties will be paid to those whose stories make the book.

For more information and to read submission guidelines, visit the website below. And tell your friends, too!

We are also accepting stories for *OMG! My Reality! Stand Up!*

www.PublishingSyndicate.com